Noticed

Dianne Leister

Contents

1.	Accalia	1
2.	Accalia	11
3.	Orchid	22
4.	Grimsley	26
5.	Grimsley	34
6.	Grimsley	43
7.	Grimsley	49
8.	Grimsley	56
9.	Orchid	63
10.	Orchid	71
11.	Grimsley	76
12.	Grimsley	80
13.	Accalia	83
14.	Accalia	90
15.	Accalia	98

Accalia

Pain.

That's all I felt. Throughout my body. The pain engulfed me like water from the ocean. No matter how much I twisted and turned, it never went away.

I felt the sticks from the ground dig into my skin, ripping at my clothing even more, and igniting the pain even more. Dirt flew into my mouth and the more I tried to spit it out, the more it came back in.

I opened my mouth in a silent scream as my vocal chords stopped working altogether and closed up as if I'm losing my voice completely.

I squeezed my eyes shut, hoping the pain will stop if I somehow faint or become unconscious. I felt as though my body was expanding, almost as if my organs and bones were becoming too big for my body.

Thinking this is the end of me, I start thinking about my family. How before Chloe was born, I was their little angel. My mom often called me "little wolf" and would always give me wolf stuffed animals or pictures to hang in my room.

That all ended when Chloe was born a year later.

I was beyond enthusiastic when my mom first brought her home. I wanted to hold her, show her my favorite white wolf with beautiful silver eyes, read her my storybooks about princesses, play with her, just be able to spend time with her.

I quickly learned that would never happen.

Whenever I asked my mom if I could hold her, she would simply tell me 'no' and turn her back on me or walk away, cooing at Chloe while she does it. I would ask my dad if I could go with him and her wherever they're going, he would just say 'no' and close the door, leaving me and my mom who only watches tv or clean around the house. When I tried showing her my white wolf, my mom ripped it out of my hands and dragged me by the collar of my shirt out of her room. Once out, she screamed at me, claiming I was trying to scare her with it and accusing me of not liking her.

What truly made me stop trying was when Chloe ripped apart my white wolf.

I had snuck into the nursery room, my parents asleep in their room. Chloe was playing with some toys that my parents had just bought her. They buy her a lot of toys. They buy her so many toys that she always has a brand new one to play with the next day.

She asked me what it was and I told her it was a wolf. I told her I named the wolf Orchid and that Orchid is my favorite stuffed animal. She held out her hands, reaching for Orchid. I gently handed her Orchid, expecting her to hug her or examine her. But instead, she grabbed Orchid by the neck, and with all the strength that a toddler has, ripped her head off!

Orchid was a beaten-up stuffed animal already, as I constantly brought her everywhere with me and my mom often had to stitch her back up due to the amount of dragging or me accidentally digging my hands into the seams. Stuffing flooded out of the body and head like a waterfall and I let out a cry of alarm.

Chloe started crying because of my scream and I quickly grabbed Orchid, trying to figure out how to put her head back on. My parents came running into the room, they saw me and Chloe with tears in our eyes, mine from my ripped stuffed animal and Chloe's from confusion and my scream.

I held out Orchid's body and head, crying about how Chloe ripped her head off while Chloe just cried.

My mom rushed over to Chloe to calm her down while my dad swiped me up and took me to my room. Expecting him to examine Orchid, I held her up to him. He grabbed her body and head and threw them in my trash bin! He screamed at me about how I did it and was trying to blame Chloe, telling me I need to start behaving myself or he'll send me to an orphanage and leave me there.

I quickly quieted down to a small sniffle and he told me I am not allowed to leave my room or play with anything or anyone for a month. He stomped out of my room, slamming the door behind him. Leaving me in my room, sniffling.

I grabbed Orchid from the trash bin, almost all her stuffing was completely gone. I didn't know how to sew as my mom said I was too young to use a needle steadily. Tears fall onto the eyes of the wolf as I can no longer hold them in anymore as I hug Orchid's body and head close to me.

My mom comes into my room only three times a day, giving me food that can barely fill me and help keep me full at night. I attempted to sneak out of my room once for food, but my mom quickly caught me as she's a light sleeper and threatened to send me to an orphanage as well or to ground me even longer.

I asked if I'm allowed to leave to use the bathroom, but my parents said no. So I was forced to use my trash bin. It was both disgusting and humiliating, especially when my parents started complaining about the smell and finally agreed to let me out to use the bathroom, but only an hour after every meal and nothing more.

I often heard Chloe laughing and playing with her toys or my parents. I was always too scared to open my door and peak out, so I only listened. Sometimes I would hear the door shutting and then silence. I'd never dared to peak out of my room for fear my mom or dad would see me and send me to an orphanage.

It was like that for my entire childhood and up to where I am now.

Even though a month was up, my parents never bothered to tell me anything or take me anywhere with them. When I first left my room, they were all watching a movie. I snuck into the kitchen to grab food and when no one was screaming at me, that's when I realized I was forgotten.

I started staying only in my room, never leaving unless necessary. I had to teach myself and watch my mom do chores around the house to be able to learn how to take care of myself.

I started to sneak out at night when I was able to find enough money around the house to spend on things that I want or need such as clothes or food other than the tiny entrees Chloe insists on eating despite the fact our parents can barely afford it.

I was able to let out a scream this time as a sharp knife of pain runs through me and even screaming feels like my vocals are being torn out.

I try to shut my eyes even harder, trying to ease some of the pain by remembering things that made me happy such as being able to figure out how to sew correctly and reattaching Orchid's head back on or listening to the wolves howl during the night.

We live in a very foresty area where there's a lot of wolves who are often spotted near the border of the forests, just watching people.

As suddenly as the pain came, it was gone.

I let out a small, but hoarse gasp as if I've been yelling at the top of my lungs for an hour straight. I slowly opened my eyes to see everything from a different perspective.

Everything was so much clearer! It was almost as if I had perfect vision, but I was also able to see far away, farther than I've ever been able to see.

I pick up on sounds that I never heard before either. I could hear a squirrel that was at least a mile away talking to itself and I could hear the hopping of a rabbit miles away, but it sounded as though it were right next to me.

I slowly get up, careful to not cause any more pain to myself. When I finally stood, I quickly realized that I was feeling the forest floor on not just my shoes, but my actual feet! But what was even stranger, was that it felt as though I felt the floor on four different feet.

Scared of what I may see, I slowly looked down and saw that my once legs and feet, were now the legs of some sort of mammal and paws!

My legs and paws were covered in white fur with tiny streaks of black, making it look dirtier than it was. I saw that I now had four legs and four paws! Not only that but a tail! I slowly moved my head to look behind me and saw that I had the body of some sort of large dog or wolf. I had white fur cover my entire body that also had the small black streaks, making it look dirty.

I let out a gasp that came out as a small whimper.

I saw a small lake a few feet away from me and hesitatingly took a small step towards it, not sure what would happen if I did take a step. I was a bit wobbly at first, but soon got a better balance and was able to slowly walk towards the lake.

Scared of what I may see, I closed my eyes and leaned my head towards the lake.

I slowly opened my eyes to see a wolf's head staring straight back at me. The same gasp came out as a whimper as I stared at my reflection.

I looked exactly like Orchid! I had her silver eyes and white fur, but I still had the black streaks that made the fur dirtier looking.

It's about time you shifted, said a voice.

I immediately whipped around to look behind me and saw no one. I frantically searched around, trying to figure out where that voice came from.

I'm your wolf silly! Said the voice again. I then realized the voice was inside my mind!

"Who...who are you?" I asked in my mind, terrified for an answer. Am I going insane? Am I dreaming?

I'm Orchid. I'm your wolf! Didn't your parents tell you about me? Or at least the fact you're a werewolf?"

"A-a what?! Werewolf?! Werewolves don't exist!"

Of course we do! After all, you just shifted into a wolf!

"Wait...so I'm not dreaming?"

Of course not! Didn't your parents tell you about you being a werewolf? Or anything at all?

"No. They never told me anything. They never tell me anything." Orchid grew silent. I called her name a couple of times, but she didn't answer.

I looked down at my reflection again and tried to think of a logical explanation for this. I couldn't possibly be a werewolf! I'm not a big meat eater, I don't feel any different when there's a full moon, and I don't feel connected to anyone or anything.

Accalia, because you and I are connected now, I can hear and see your thoughts and vice versa. I looked at your memories so then I can know you better and understand why Luna decided to make me connected to you, said Orchid finally.

"Luna? Who's Luna?"

"Luna is the moon goddess or werewolf goddess for us werewolves. We worship her and in return, she turns your soul into thirds. One third being you, the other your wolf, and the other being your mate. Us werewolves have what is called a mate. A soulmate. You will know when you meet your mate. Meeting your mate is the best thing to ever happen to a werewolf. Because they're a third of your soul," said Orchid.

"Hold on. You're telling me that I'm a werewolf and that my soul is split into thirds? And that another werewolf is one of the thirds of my soul?"

It doesn't have to be another werewolf. It can be human and in very rare cases, another full-on wolf. And yes. You're a werewolf.

"Are vampires real then?"

Yes. However, they live in cities where more people are around. Werewolves and vampires never interact with one another due to the different environments we live in and the life requirements we need.

"Why didn't my parents ever say anything to me?"

I honestly don't know. You would have to ask them. I can sense your mother's wolf, but your father is human.

"How am I a werewolf then if my father is human?"

It all depends on genetics. Because you got more of your mother's genetics, you are a full werewolf. Unlike your sister. She got more of your father's genetics, so she is more human than a werewolf. But there is the possibility that there's a tiny sliver of a werewolf in her. She just needs more werewolf genetics to help her fully shift.

"Why don't you call them your parents and sister too?"

"Because to us wolves, our parents are Luna. She gives birth to us. The human counterpart gives birth to the human counterpart of werewolves. So while you may call them mother and father, I see them only as alpha, luna, which is the female alpha, beta, werewolf, omega, or human. Also, from what I see in your memories, I wouldn't consider them family." Orchid's explanation and reason shock me. While my family never acknowledged me, no matter what I did, I still saw them as a family because they're who gave me life and a place to live.

They were the only people I had in my life.

"Orchid, do you know if my father knows about this? About werewolves and everything," I asked Orchid.

Yes. He knows fully well that someone who he married is a werewolf and that his children may be werewolves as well. It's hard for mates to keep secrets from one another."

~

After finally wrapping my head around what just happened and having Orchid explain things to me at least twice, I finally returned home, naked due to my clothes being ripped apart when I shifted. Orchid told me it's normal to lose clothing while shifting as there's no clothing or fabric currently that can stretch enough and shrink enough to fit a wolf form and human form at the same time.

Thankfully no one saw me and my house was at the border of a forest, so I was able to easily find it after following the trail that I was using when I was going on a walk into the forest. When I snuck back inside, I saw that no one was home which meant they probably left somewhere that Chloe wanted to go to, most likely the mall where all her friends go every weekend.

I quickly took a shower and when I got out, I saw that they returned and that my mom was making one of Chloe's expensive and tiny entrees for dinner. I saw my dad watching tv on the couch and Chloe was nowhere in sight, probably in her room, trying on the new clothes she got or showing off the new makeup she got to her friends who weren't able to go.

"Mom. I have a question for you," I said to my mother. But like always, my mom simply ignores me and continues working on dinner.

"Mom, why didn't you tell me I'm a werewolf?" My mom stopped working for a split second but quickly went back to what she was doing.

"Mom. Orchid told me everything about being a werewolf. About Luna, mates, werewolf packs. Why aren't we in one?" Once again I'm answered with silence and my mom ignoring me.

I glanced over at my dad who is still watching tv and doesn't show any sign of listening or even acknowledge my existence.

Chloe eventually came walking into the kitchen, wearing what appeared to be an expensive necklace and earrings along with a designer shirt.

My dad compliments her and finally, my mom turned around. However, it's only to look at Chloe like she always does.

Taking this as my chance, I asked my mom why she didn't say anything about being a werewolf to me again.

"Oh, mom and dad never told you anything?" Chloe says in her false surprised voice while putting a small delicate hand up to her mouth, obviously showing off the new ring she also got as well.

"They told you?!" I quickly said.

"Of course! They told me that next year, I'll shift into a BEAUTIFUL wolf and the next-in-line alpha of the Tourmaline pack, which is the royal werewolf pack, of course, will choose me as his mate as we were born to be together!" She throws her hand with the ring up to her head and pretends to fall over as if she were about to faint and fall into the arms of her charming prince.

"I wish you the best," I muttered as I walked out of the kitchen and to my room.

"Your mother's wolf was begging her to acknowledge you. She was scolding her for never saying anything to you and was fighting her for control so she could tell you everything and show you the love she should have shown you when you were little," said Orchid once we're back in my room.

"Why should it matter? The damage was already done. Also, don't bother trying to wake me up for dinner. It's nothing good. We'll hit the gas station for breakfast before school tomorrow." I said as I threw myself onto my bed and went to sleep.

Little to my knowledge, a wolf had run-up to my window and stared up at it longingly.

Accalia

I let out a sigh as I looked up at my high school. The high school is small and is made of eroded stone, giving it a more rustic or ancient look. Ivy climbs up the walls of the building and even goes inside the school through openings of either the stone or windows due to the fact the school has no actual windows, but rather openings. There are three stories to the high school, the first being a basement that's underground and is used for gym or any athletic activities such as a weight room.

The second floor is mainly used for quieter and less hands-on classes such as English, Math, and History. All the hands-on classes are on the third floor so then they'll have the roof to use for any outdoor needs such as the robotics, music, science, or art classes.

There's a very small dirt parking lot as a lot of people rather walk to places than drive because of the noise and smoke that a car makes. All the roads in the town are dirt roads that were mainly created through trucks driving to and from the town as it's a dead-end and only forest beyond the town.

I look at the many teens talking to their friends or even making out with their partner while their friends tease or insult them about it. No one bothered to try and strike a conversation with me or even look in my direction as I am the outcast of the town.

All because of Chloe.

When Chloe was born, my parents didn't hesitate to show her to everyone in the town and brag about the things she did or how beautiful she was. Whenever someone would ask about me or even ask for a comparison of me and her, my parents would immediately go quiet and quickly change the topic to either Chloe or anything else aside from me. Thus, leading people to decide that I'm not worth their breath and started to ignore me as well.

"Why isn't anyone coming up to you or saying anything to you? I'm getting a lot of wolves asking me why their human counterpart is completely ignoring us," Orchid breaks me out of my thoughts.

"Because we're the outcast. We're the person who is a simple background character that no one bothers to acknowledge or waste their breath on. We're nothing Orchid," I said in a monotone voice. "And what do you mean "other wolves?" Are there more werewolves here?" I added in a confused voice.

Yes. While the human counterpart cannot sense if another werewolf is around, we wolves can. We're able to communicate with one another without our human counterpart knowing and can do it if we're within a certain radius of one another. We can even do it if our human counterpart is asleep but we're not. Almost everyone here is a werewolf. Those who aren't just simply haven't turned 18 which is when you first shift," explained Orchid. "And I wish you stopped calling yourself that and looking down on yourself. Just because you're forced to live in your sister's shadow, that doesn't mean you won't reach greater heights than her. If anything, she'll become a stripper or prostitute because she can't do anything. Trust me Accalia. Those who rise during school will most likely fall when they're thrust into the real world." I just smiled at what Orchid just said about Chloe and agreed with her.

I walked through the open oak doors and headed for the stairs to my first class which was Honors Algebra II. Since there was still 30 minutes until school started, everyone was either outside socializing or inside and frantically working on homework that they've forgotten or studied for a test that they have.

I saw Chloe by one of the classrooms, flirting with a senior who was also in my algebra class. I could tell she was simply flirting with him so then he would do her homework and she could go skip class later to make out with some random teen or go with her friends to the mall again to buy stupidly expensive things.

"Why does she even bother coming to school if she's just going to be skipping it and not listen to the teachers when she is here?" I wonder to myself.

Probably to find her next poor victim whom she'll make out with only to have them realize their mistake later when they remember that they're a werewolf who just hasn't shifted yet.

"Hey Orchid, you told me almost everyone here is a werewolf. Do you mean that..."

That this entire town is made up of a werewolf population? Yup. There are only a few humans here, counting your father, and they already know about the existence of werewolves. They're mainly doctors for humans in case the town gets a human case instead of a werewolf one since our bodies are different.

"Does that mean there's an alpha here? And that this entire town could just be one pack?"

Yes. The entire town is made up of one pack with an alpha who lives farther down in the forest. He has what's called an alpha voice in which he can use to get any wolf of his pack to completely submit to him and do what he tells them to do. He can make someone spill all their secrets or even forcibly make them shift if he so chooses. However, his alpha voice won't work on wolves outside of the pack"

"What about the lunas? And can't there be female alphas?"

If you mean luna when you say female alpha, yes. Although, it's very rare to have a female have complete control of a wolfpack. While the alpha and luna are considered equal in power, they're powerful in different forms. The alpha has the most power when it comes to giving commands or having training. Luna is more powerful when it comes to pups or children along with any medical situations. However, both have equal power over the overall pack.

While thinking about what Orchid was telling me, I felt myself slam into what felt like a wall. While I was trying to clear my mind, Orchid suddenly went silent and it felt as though she were either trying to tell me something but couldn't or leap out of me and onto the wall that we just ran into.

"Why are you suddenly so excited? What's so exciting about a wall?" I asked confused and silently annoyed as she was making me feel super weird and as if my heart were about to jump out of my chest.

"Accalia...we didn't run into a wall...we ran into our mate," Orchid said very quietly almost as if she were to speak any louder, she would break something or destroy the world itself.

"Mate? What's a mate?" Before she could answer, I inhaled and the most amazing scent hit me. It smelled of the forest after rainfall, but not the heavy mildew smell. But rather fresh rain that didn't rain hard enough to cause the mildew smell.

I looked up to see who Orchid was talking about and that's when my heart completely stopped.

I was looking at Grimsley Canis.

In other words, my mate was the son of the most powerful person in the town. Making him the top boy in society.

Both mine and his breath seem to be caught in our throats as we stare at one another's eyes. He has dark, almost black hair that falls into his random strands because he doesn't bother to brush it or do anything with it. I'm having to resist the urge to reach up and move the strands from his blue eyes that almost appear as though there are amber specks in them, almost like flecks of gold in the ocean. He has bronze skin from being out in the sun so much along with a strong build, most likely from working out or doing whatever rich people's sons do. He easily towers over me as I'm 5'2" and he's at least 6 feet tall, making me barely reach his shoulders or chest.

We continue to stare at one another for who knows how long, a long-range of emotions flickering through his eyes. Amazement, confusion, surprise, disappointment, etc.

"Disappointment? Why would he be disappointed in meeting me?" I wondered to myself.

"You aren't Chloe," he says in a deep and confused voice.

"I'm not Chloe? What do you mean by that?" I find myself asking before thinking of any other response such as just walking away and screaming questions at Orchid about mates.

"Zarik told me he sensed a new presence and made me run. I found your house and I smelled your scent. You're my mate. But I thought it was Chloe because Luna couldn't have paired me with such an outcast," he said.

"Zarik? Whos Zarik?"

"My wolf. He didn't tell me who it was. Refused to. Now I know why. He was trying to save me from disappointment."

"Disappointment? How am I a disappointment to you already? We've never talked or even crossed paths ever before. And do you even know how old Chloe is? She's 17, a year younger than me. So she couldn't have possibly shifted already," I find myself saying, unable to control it.

All the bent up anger, sadness, disappointment, stress, everything. It finally comes flying out.

"I know. But I figured she either just turned 18 or was about to. I can't have you as my mate. I'm sorry."

"What? I don't even know what a mate is."

"I. Grimsley Canis. Reject you. Accalia Lupus as my mate."

"What do you mean-" My sentence is suddenly caught off as I feel as though my heart literally fell into a thousand pieces and was now piercing through my lungs and falling into my stomach where it pierced my body even farther. I felt as though something inside of me was being ripped apart and I let out a choked cry of pain as I felt myself drop down to my knees and Grimsley's feet.

I feel his gaze on me but don't bother looking up. I feel tears sting at my eyes like glass shards being pressed into my eyes and forced down my cheeks, leaving a trail. I feel Orchid go dim like a fire that has run out of fuel to burn off of and is now only relying on itself to keep going.

I feel him pick me up which both feels warm and comforting, but at the same time, cold and unbearable. I feel him place me on the floor somewhere but I can't tell where. I hear him say something but it's as if I've suddenly gone deaf and can't hear a thing. I don't bother tearing my gaze from anything but the tiled floor underneath me, even though I can feel him asking me to meet his gaze and listen to him.

Eventually, he leaves, closing the door behind him. I am no longer holding any of my things as I feel as though my entire body has gone completely limp and useless. I felt as though I had no use for life anymore. What if I were to die right now. No one would care. Everyone would live happier lives after the funeral. They'll all pretend to miss me. Pretend to remember all the memories that they've shared with me.

Only to forget me once again.

I make a weak attempt at calling out to Orchid to which I get no response. I stare at the tiled wall in front of me. It's dirty and empty. It seems to have no meaning in life, almost as if it's given up long ago and now only resides in what I'm assuming is a bathroom for teachers since there was only one toilet and sink.

"I feel like that tile," I think to myself. I look over to the side to see a window opening. Since I was on the third floor, I only really saw the ground beyond the school, tops of trees, and the sky. How free and alive it looked.

How promising it looked.

Without thinking, I get up. I feel myself opening the door of the bathroom and ignoring everyone around me as they do to me, I go to the door to the roof and open it. It closes behind me and I go to the edge of the roof.

I can tell school hasn't started as there were still a lot of people outside, socializing or making out. I look beyond them and at the promising forest. The forest looked so welcoming and warm.

It looked alive.

Wanting to feel that warmth, I go to the edge of the roof.

I looked down one last time.

I see Grimsley talking with Chloe who gladly accepts the conversation and responses by flirting. I feel jealousy run through my veins and for a moment, I felt myself wanting to jump off the roof and run towards them, yelling at Chloe to get away from him.

That feeling quickly fades however and is replaced by the cold and lifelessness.

I look at the forest again. It's currently in the middle of autumn, so the trees still have plenty of their leaves which are beautiful colors of oranges, yellows, reds, and golden. It all looks so welcoming and warm.

I yearn for that warmth.

Without thinking, I stepped off of the ledge.

I first feel the crisp air blow at me as I fall, accepting my faith. Then, suddenly, something within me changes.

It wasn't painful like I thought. But rather, warm. I allowed it to engulf me and instead of hitting the ground and simply falling, I'm running.

I don't bother to look at any of the shocked faces of anyone and I ignore the questions and comments shouted at me. I don't bother to look at Grimsley or Chloe as I run past them, I just simply keep running.

I enjoy the feeling of the air on my fur, filtering through it like how water does in a strainer. I take in all the smells of the forest and allow them to engulf me. I ran to the lake where I first saw my reflection and leap into it.

I feel the water splash against my fur and hit my skin, freezing me instantly. But I didn't mind. Unlike the cold and lifelessness, this was soothing and calming. I allowed myself to just simply stand there, allowing the water to splash all around me and engulf me.

When I finally walked out, I found a rock in the sun in which I just lay on and allow the sun to dry me off while warming me.

I soon drift off and into a deep slumber.

~

I wake up with a gasp. I quickly realize that I'm in my wolf form and that I'm in the forest. I quickly roll over so I'm laying on my stomach and looking at the sky. It's nighttime.

Trying to remember why I'm here or what even happened, it all comes rushing back like a tidal wave during high tide. Finding out Grimsley is my mate, having him reject me, the cold and lifelessness within me, Trying to kill me.

"Orchid, What happened?!" I quickly think, hoping she'll answer.

"After Grimsley rejected you, I went into shock. It's when a wolf completely blanks out and almost cuts itself from the human counterpart, unable to reply to you unless I try my hardest and I almost ripped myself from you by mistake. When I finally came out of it, the next thing I knew you were stepping off a ledge. I quickly forced control over your body and made you shift, saving your life possibly. I had us run here where you can rest and calm down in peace. Accalia. Please. Promise me you'll never do that again." I can tell Orchid is almost in tears at the memory of what had just happened and I feel tears start to drip out of my eyes like tiny raindrops falling from a thinning rain cloud.

"I promise Orchid. But I honestly don't know what came over me. It's almost as if someone or something took control over me and without thinking, I wanted to do that. But please. Explain everything to me. Mates, rejection, you taking control. Everything."

Mates, like I said, is a third of your soul. When you complete the mating ritual with your mate, you feel as though you're finally whole, as though if you were to die right now, you would be completely fine with it because you feel as though you fulfilled your life. Mates are everything to us werewolves. Without our mate, we are unable to function properly. We become easily irritated, easy-tempered, and just cold in general. Mates are like the light at the end of a dark tunnel.

"Is both the human and wolf part connected?"

It all depends on who you ask. While Luna does create the mates for the wolves, she's not the one who decides who their human counterpart is. Some claim that both the human and wolf counterparts are bound to be together through their souls while others say that without the wolf, you might never have met your mate and have a false feeling of fullness.

"What Grimsley did. Reject us. What was that?"

While it's rare for a mate to reject the other, it does happen as you just saw and felt. Rejecting your mate for whatever reason means rejecting your fullness and happiness. The rejector may not feel anything. They may feel guilt, sympathy for their mate, it all depends on the rejector. The rejected, such as you, feels what you felt. Depression, loneliness, a loss to live anymore. Often the rejected will attempt what you just attempted.

Committing suicide.

Sometimes the wolf can come back from the shock in time to prevent it, but most of the time, the wolf has also given up and will allow their human counterpart to kill both of them. In rare cases, a wolf will reject the rejector's wolf, thus leading to that wolf to go into depression and attempt to take control of their human counterpart and attempt suicide themselves."

"Is there any way mates could get back together?"

Yes. If they complete the mating ritual like normal, then they will feel fulfilled and happy once again. The only way for two mates to get back together is through them completing the mating ritual. Some claim that there is another way to get to two mates back together without having to do the mating ritual, but almost no one knows that way or how to even do it. Or what it even is for that matter."

"What about taking control? What is that?"

Taking control is where the wolf takes complete control of the body. If a wolf is in complete control, it will act upon pure instinct and not reasoning or anything. If its instinct is telling it to kill someone, it will do it. If it's telling it to do the mating ritual right where it and its mate is, it'll do it immediately, attacking anyone who dares try to disturb it. Having a wolf take over can be deadly not only for itself but others around it as it can easily become unpredictable.

"What's the mating process?"

The mating process is where the two mates decide to have sex. During it, when the male is ready to finish, it will bite the skin that is between the neck and shoulder, marking their mate as theirs. The bite is completed when the male finishes. Just like the male, when the female is about to finish, she will bite the male in the same spot that he bites her or vice versa and when she finishes, the bite is complete. Thus, the ritual has been completed and the only thing that can rip them apart is death."

Orchid

- -

Upon making sure Accalia was completely asleep, I went into my mind.

I howled for Zarik to meet me at the lake in which Accalia first found out she shifted and within seconds, he agreed.

In my mind, I ran down the black void, bare of nothing but darkness. Eventually, I feel my paws hit something wet and the lake soon morphed in front of me.

Everything was exactly how I remembered it. From how the stones were placed on the ground to how many leaves were on a tree. The water was crystal clear and I saw the full moon reflecting upon it, making it look as though there was a reversed world within the lake.

I heard a small purr and turned around to see Zarik.

Zarik's fur was a blend of white, grey, and black. White covered the bottom of his muzzle and a bit of the top, having grey and black cover the rest of his face. His ears are bordered with black fur and grey-white fur between. He mainly had white and grey fur on his chest and his legs were mainly covered by black and grey fur while the inside was mainly silver and white.

His back was covered mainly in black and grey fur while the top of his tail was covered in black-grey fur and white fur at the bottom. He had icy blue eyes and a muscular body clearly from being from a line of alphas.

I stepped out of the water and he met me halfway towards. He immediately nuzzled my neck and I almost forgot why I had asked him to meet me. He smelled of the forest and power and just like Accalia with Grimsley, he easily towered over me, having me barely reach up to his head.

His purring got louder as he nuzzled deeper into my fur to the point his whole body was vibrating with it. I gently nuzzled him back, trying to enjoy the moment and feeling of him against me.

But I sadly couldn't.

"Zarik," I finally said. He just hummed in response, clearly not bothering to listen to me and rather enjoy the moment as we both know this will probably be the last time we will be able to be together.

"I have something to tell you...I don't think you'll like it either," I tried saying again.

"Mmm, what is it?" He finally says, still deep in my fur.

"I'm so sorry Zarik." I pulled away from him, causing much confusion for him. He whimpers a bit and tries to move closer towards me, to which I stepped away from him.

"Sorry for what? I should be the one apologizing for how Grimsley acted today. He should have never done that," Zarik says with a slight growl at his human counterpart's name.

"It's actually about that," I said sadly. "After Grimsley rejected Accalia, she decided she can no longer take the ignoring or neglect from anyone. She decided she's going to run away. She wants me to take over so she can forever be alone and attempt to forget everything. She plans on shifting into her wolf form and staying in it forever."

Zarik just stares at me in complete shock and worry. He just stood there frozen like a statue.

"Orchid, you couldn't possibly have agreed to any of that! Who knows what will happen to Accalia if she just lives off of raw animals and drinking from lakes or rivers," Zarik quickly says, clearly more worried about me than Accalia.

"I'm sorry Zarik. But you didn't see her memories as I did. You don't understand the hardships and neglect she had to go through throughout her life while Chloe is alive. You saw what she tried to do after being rejected by Grimsley. I can't have her go through anything like that or the neglect anymore. I don't like the conditions, but they're better than having her live a life full of misery," I answered sadly.

"What are you saying Orchid?" Asked Zarik, clearly starting to realize what I'm about to say.

"I'm sorry Zarik. Truly. I love you dearly and I hope you can understand why I'm doing this."

"Orchid..." Zarik said in a growl, but also a worried and scared voice, realizing what I'm about to say.

"Zarik. I. Orchid. Wolf of Accalia Lupus. Reject you. Zarik. Wolf of Grimsley Canis. As my mate. Please Zarik, understand why I'm doing this." I can barely look Zarik in the eye, feeling the pain and shock radiate off of him as he tries to figure out what to say or do.

"Orchid..." He could barely speak and I heard his voice break as he attempted to talk.

"I'm so sorry Zarik. But please. Try to move on. It'll be best for both of us. Goodbye Zarik." I slowly turned away from Zarik, begging that he doesn't make this any harder in trying to follow me or call out after me.

He thankfully didn't call out or chase after me. But I felt his saddened gaze on me the entire time I walked away from him.

I quickly shut my eyes, trying to hide the tears that were forming, trying to stay strong for not only me and Accalia but him as well.

Grimsley

I woke up in the middle of the night with a gasp. I felt as though knives were being shoved into my chest and needles were scrapping all over my body.

"Zarik?! Why do I feel like this?!" I quickly called for my wolf, hoping for a response.

Silence.

"Zarik?" I tried it again. Still nothing.

I felt the worst pain ever. It was ten times worse than when I first shifted or when my father would hit me for misbehaving or not owning up to my duties as next-in-line-alpha. I let out a hoarse gasp as I felt tears of pain spring into my eyes which I quickly wiped away, hoping no one saw that weakness from me.

"Grimsley? Are you okay? Luca alerted me that he felt Zarik's presence leave and then come back super depressed, almost as if your mate died or something. What's going on?" I heard my second youngest brother, Marshall knocking at my door with a confused and concerned voice.

Grinding my teeth against one another, trying to fight through the pain, and show no weakness, I do my best to tell him in a calm and monotone voice that I'm fine.

"You might be brothers through blood, but that doesn't mean your brothers through the soul. Anyone of your brothers can easily turn against you when you have your back turned and you won't even notice it. Always be on guard when it comes to them. All brothers end up turning against one another." Father's voice rings through my ears, reminding me to be wary of Marshall as he is the closest to me through age which means he can easily overpower me at any point if he so chooses.

While my other two brothers, Grant and Valentine don't pose as too much of a threat, I can never be too careful with them. Grant appears to be the most honest and trustworthy as he's good at keeping secrets and isn't afraid of lying if it means protecting those who he cares about or bending the truth if someone comes too close to a secret that he knows.

Valentine, on the other hand, is still too naive to notice anything. He does whatever he's told without a second thought and just simply tries to stay on everyone's good side by telling jokes or simply just being friendly towards anyone and everyone. While he is naive and innocent, something tells me that he knows more than he's putting out as he hinted at how he knows certain things that no one should know. When asked about what he knows, he just simply goes back to being naive and wanting to be friends.

Marshall poses the biggest threat to me. While he is blunt and plays fair, that doesn't mean he doesn't avoid confronting anyone and even getting into fights with others. It's constantly close calls between me and him when we're paired against one another and he appears to rather use psychology rather than strength in his fights. Choosing to mess with his opponent's mind rather than trying to fight them physically. He also has a strong brain when it comes to medical situations or science in general, making him an even bigger threat as he knows how to manipulate people to be on his side and how to slip poison in a drink.

"You sure about that Grimsley? You don't sound okay to me. Luca is trying to get into contact with Zarik but can't. Did something happen between the two of you?" Marshall breaks me out of my thoughts and I instantly remember my father's words.

"I'm fine." I snapped, hoping to sound more confident than I am. "Just go back to bed." I pray for Marshall to listen to me and to just leave, not bringing it up to anyone while at it. Especially father.

If father were to catch wind of me showing weakness, especially to Marshall or anyone, he wouldn't hesitate to take me to the training room and fight me. Telling me to prove my dominance to him and that I'm worthy of the alpha position more than any of my other brothers. Especially Marshall.

Mother would simply watch the entire fight, never bothering to say anything and only stepping in when she believes my father is taking it too far.

My mother's an interesting werewolf. She knows more than anyone else in the pack and she's the only one my father willingly bends to. She's the head medic of the pack and when modern medication doesn't seem to work, she always resorts to using herbs and weird and ancient rituals that shouldn't work but do. Some claim that she's a part witch as there is a history of witches and werewolves mating and having pups. However, she appears to have no bloodline of it as her entire family who has been recorded were all werewolves.

"Grimsley. I know you'll hate me even more than you already do, but I don't believe you. You have two choices now. You can either open this door and let me check on you or I will have to force myself in. It's your choice," Marshall breaks me out of my thoughts once again.

"I said, I'm fine," I used my developing alpha voice this time. I can tell he flinched at this sudden tone of my voice, but because my alpha voice hasn't fully developed and is now reaching its limit to the point where I need to be officially declared alpha, it doesn't work on him.

"Guess I'm breaking down your door then. Don't stand anywhere near it." Not giving me any time to reply or even move, I hear Marshall backing away from my door and then ramming into it with his shoulder, easily breaking the lock, but not the actual door somehow as it flies and slams into the wall before slamming back closed, leaving me and Marshall in complete darkness.

Officially annoyed and pain forgotten, I attempt to flash my wolf eyes at him to prove my point and authority to him only to feel my eyes strain against my skull. Confused, I try this again only to have the same result.

"Zarik? Where are you?" I tried asking once again. Still no response. "Zarik?" Now I'm worried and confused. Zarik still refuses to reply to me.

"Grimsley? What is happening? Luca tells me he's unable to get any response from Zarik and that he can't even find Zarik anywhere," Marshall says worriedly.

For a second, I almost considered telling him everything that had happened today since he no longer goes to school as he was able to graduate early. About Accalia, rejecting her, hanging out with Chloe, seeing her jump off the roof only to shift into the most beautiful wolf I've ever seen and see her run into the woods. Nowhere to be seen.

I suddenly felt a jump as if my heart skipped a beat and I immediately realized it was Zarik.

"Zarik!" Quickly jumping to the chance to finally get a response from him. "Where have you been? Why are you doing this?"

"Don't. Talk. To. Me. Ever. Again." Is all Zarik says to me before completely blocking me out.

I let out a gasp as the sudden pain of knives and needles digging into my skin returned as I finally realized what it's from.

Zarik is tearing himself from me.

"Grimsley! What is happening! Luca tells me that Zarik is tearing himself away from you and going as far as possible from you!" Marshall almost yells frantically.

"You don't think I've realized that?! And keep your voice down! No one knows about this, you hear me?!" I growled at him, staring him dead in the eye as I said this.

Marshall immediately closed his mouth and just stared at me for a bit before saying, "I will not tell anyone. But if father starts asking me, Grant, or Valentine about what's wrong with you, I won't hesitate to tell him of this night. Good-night Grimsley." Marshall swiftly turns around and slams the door behind him, having it rattle against the doorframe for a bit before finally settling down.

Once he was gone, I frantically got out of bed and into my bathroom which was across the room from my bed. I flick on the light, ignoring the sudden pain from my eyes from the sudden brightness, and go straight towards my sink and mirror.

I look at my reflection. Taking in my dark, almost black hair, bronze skin from the amount of running in the forest I had to do while school was out, and my blue eyes with specks of amber, something that I inherited from my father which is supposed to signify the next alpha.

I look at my reflection deeply, trying to find any difference in my appearance from what Zarik is doing to me. Aside from unable to get my wolf eyes to flash, nothing looked different on me. I backed up a bit so I could look at my full body and see if there was any difference there. There was none.

Running a hand through my hair, messing it up, even more, I walked out to my bedroom and looked around. The wall facing outside is completely glass, giving me an entire view of the forest and the sunset. I could see all the tops of the trees in the forest and if I looked hard enough, I can sometimes spot owls flying through the trees or even bats flying, swooping down to grab food.

My walls are painted a dark navy blue, making it even darker with my bed in the center of the wall. My floor is covered with black wood and I have a black rug next to my bed and in front of my nightstand which has a lamp, an alarm, and nothing else on it.

On the wall with my bathroom, I have a flat-screen tv hooked up on the wall with a tv stand underneath that doesn't have anything on it. In the corner next to the window wall, is my walk-in closet which I keep closed a lot. My room is very bare to say for when I'm borrowing weight lifting equipment from the training room.

Going to the middle of my room, I quickly looked out the window to make sure no one was watching me before turning back around and focusing on shifting. I think of my wolf form, the blend of grey, white, and black along with the icy blue eyes. I think of my height and strength when I'm in my wolf form and how I'm running through the forest, feeling my paws crunch on the fallen leaves during the autumn season.

I feel the heat starting to radiate off of me and I grind my teeth together, preparing for the sudden change in body form and power. Nothing happens. Confused, I attempted at it again only to get the same result. Nothing. I keep trying for five more minutes but with the same result.

Now frustrated, I attempt to call out for Zarik to which I get no response or reaction.

I look at my alarm clock which reads 2:30 AM in red glowing numbers and letters. Letting out a frustrated growl, I stalk over to my bed and sit on it, trying to think of what could be causing Zarik to act this way. "Is it because of Accalia?" I finally concluded. At the mention of Accalia's name, I feel Zarik immediately rise in response.

"So it's Accalia that's causing you to be like this. Why? You never acted this way towards anyone or anything before. The closet was when we kissed Chloe." At the mention of Chloe's name, Zarik let out a feral growl that I felt rattle throughout my entire body.

"Don't you mean, you?" Zarik growled at me. "I was beyond happy when we finally found our mate and your stupid ass ruined it by rejecting what was supposed to be our other half and true partner. So why am I acting up then? Huh, Grimsley?" Zarik continues to growl at me.

"You weren't like this all day. You were quiet sure, but that was it. What else is making you cause this?"

"Maybe it's the fact that Orchid rejected me! She told me to meet her at the lake and I did. Only to have her apologize for YOUR mistake and then reject me! So not only did you ruin the best person ever for you but the best wolf ever for me. Good job, human."

This takes me completely by shock. While it's rare, but not unheard of for wolves to reject one another if the human counterpart does, they're usually unable to fight off their instinct to mate with their partner wolf which is usually how mates end up doing the ritual, whether they realize it or not.

"You sure? You sure she wasn't just saying that for attention? After all, she has been ignored almost her entire life and maybe this is just some sort of arouse to try and get some attention," I tried to reason with him, for some reason not wanting to believe it myself.

"You're hopeless Grimsley. I hope someday Marshall does beat you. Maybe then you'll finally wise up and realize not everything is about power." After saying that, Zarik once again tore himself from me, bringing back the pain.

Grimsley

It's been about a week since my conversation with Zarik and it has been Hell. Because he decided to tear himself from me, I am unable to shift, heal quickly, have increased strength, eyesight, hearing, etc. And it has been showing.

Because of my now disabilities of being a werewolf, I can't easily win as I used to and I have to constantly come up with exercises on why I can't fight in my wolf form during training. While Marshall has kept his word, he doesn't bother to go any lighter on me during training and constantly gives me disapproving looks whenever I skip wolf training or come up with an excuse on why I'm unable to do wolf training.

"Grimsley. We need to talk." I heard Marshall suddenly say from the training room's bathroom. I quickly turned around to see him leaning against the door entrance, arms crossed. It's clear he locked it and kicked anyone out of the bathroom while I was taking my shower so that no one else can hear our conversation. At least he was being courteous.

"About what?" I growled, already knowing what he's about to say.

"About you lying to everyone about how Zarik had torn himself away from you. Luca finally managed to get a hold of Zarik who explained everything to him. So, you chose your pride rather than your mate huh? That's low. Even for you." In the last sentence, Marshall had his wolf eyes flash at me, showing me he was serious and that Luca is also talking.

"So you decide to talk to Luca but not me, Zarik?" I said to Zarik, hoping to get a response from him.

"Shut up human. Luca's the only other wolf I trust to talk too. You should learn to trust the right werewolves human." After saying that, I felt him immediately tear himself away from me again.

I let out a gasp of pain as I clutched onto the sink and bent over as I felt the familiar, but still painful knives and needles of pain go throughout my entire body once again as this has been going on every time I'm finally able to get a response from Zarik.

He would constantly just snap at me and tell me that I'm making all the wrong decisions or just simply come back only to leave again. Bringing back the pain every time he does decide to leave.

Marshall just watched me with monotone eyes, not allowing any sign of weakness or sympathy to be seen while he stood there. "This is what I mean Grimsley. You can't keep this rouse up forever. Father will get suspicious and start asking questions. When he does, I won't hesitate to tell him the truth," his words echo off of the tile walls of the bathroom and vibrate in my ears like a broken record player, repeating the same thing over and over again.

"You keep saying that but you haven't truly said anything to him yet," I managed to sneer through clenched teeth as I pray for the pain to end sooner rather than later.

"That's because Father isn't suspicious yet. But Grant and Valentine are. You know those two. Especially Grant. If either one of them were to find out about what's going on, they won't hesitate to report it to Father. You need to either step on your pride and just tell him or have one of us do it and have him get even madder."

"Why haven't you said anything then? You can easily take me down now and we both know Father wants the strongest son to become alpha and kill off his brothers."

"Because I don't want to be alpha!" Marshall suddenly snaps, taking me completely aback. "I much rather become the head medic than alpha. Why do you think I focus so much on studying medicine and spending all my free time in the hospital wing? I don't care about being alpha. And I don't want to kill you or any of the other brothers. Despite what Father says, we're still family and family needs to protect one another, whether it's against an enemy or themselves. You choose whether or not you decide to be your person or Father's shadow, Grimsley." When Marshall said the last sentence, I heard both him and Luca talking at once.

A feat that none of us have been able to accomplish. About to snap something at him about how he's lying or trying to manipulate me as he does to everyone, he swiftly left the bathroom, the door slowly closing behind him.

Pain is forgotten, I was about ready to go running after him when Grant came walking in. Grant just gave me a confused look and looked back at the opened door, clearly wondering what had just happened between me and Marshall.

"Don't ask," I just simply muttered to him, turning towards the mirror to dry off my hair with a towel.

"You know. You've been acting strange lately Grimsley. You aren't as strong as you used to be. What's up with that?" He casually asks, lifting himself up and onto the sink where he simply watches me. Grant was only a year younger than me while Marshall was only a few months younger. Valentine is a year younger than Grant, but due to having alpha blood running through him, he was able to shift this year while he was still 17 and not 18.

'I don't know what you're talking about," I said, trying to sound monotone to not give off any hints as Grant preys on them and easily connects the pieces.

"You sure about that older brother? When we were combating, you seemed rather...weak. Even Marshall seemed way stronger than you and it looked as though he were holding back as to not hurt you. Which is strange for him."

"I said, it's nothing," I tried using my alpha voice but couldn't because Zarik had completely torn himself away from me.

"Doesn't sound like nothing. I also get the feeling Marshall knows things that we don't. Mind filling us in older brother?"

"It's none of your concerns," I growled, hoping he'll stop prying me for information. Even though I trust him more than the other two, I still need to keep my back straight and not show any weakness towards him as he could easily turn his back on me.

"I think it would be if it involves family. Also, I've heard rumors of a girl jumping off the roof of the high school and shifting midair before running off. So far, Father nor his patrols seem to be able to find this mysterious wolf and no one knows who she is. Some claim to have seen her and you talking older brother."

"She's nothing to me," I answered quickly. Too quickly I realized. Looking up to stare Grant directly in the eyes I look for any sign of emotion that could give away his position. I saw nothing. He stared back at me with cool and collected eyes, daring me to try something.

"So you admit. You do know her?" He breathes, clearly trying to get me to show more weakness towards him.

"Why bother asking? We all know how much you prey on emotions and body language. It won't be too hard for you to find out the truth," I said in a cool and collected voice.

"I can. But. It's much more fun when the wolf just simply gives me the information. And Parks tells me he's unable to get into contact with Zarik," Grant pries for more information. "He almost can't sense him." He breathes.

Letting out a growl, I throw Grant off of the sink and onto the floor. He quickly growls back and lunges at me. We immediately become a rolling mess on the floor as we attempt to throw hits or kicks at one another, Grant seemingly becoming more and more superior as he still has his wolf connected to him.

I hear screams and yells from others around us, but no one dares separates us. I hear some running out of the bathroom, most likely to grab Father, but I was beyond enraged to care at that moment. I knew I was fighting a losing battle because Parks was offering more strength to Grant as he had almost inhuman strength and speed.I felt his claws rip at my skin and I felt my blood gush out everywhere and on the floor. Some were yelling at Grant and me to stop before alpha came, but neither one of us was about to admit defeat to the other, so we continued to roll on the ground.

"GRANT AND GRIMSLEY. STOP THIS IMMEDIATELY!" Our Father's alpha voice rang throughout the bathroom and echoed off of the tiles, making it feel as though the entire room was shaking as if there were an earthquake.

Feeling Parks weakened by our Father and even Zarik weakened by it, we immediately pull ourselves up to face our father, never staring him directly in the eye.

"BOTH OF YOU. IN MY OFFICE. NOW!" Not bothering to make sure we're following him, he immediately turns around and stalks out of the bathroom. Keeping our heads up and looking directly in front of us, we followed him.

Father's office was in the center of the packhouse with a window wall behind his desk that faces the training grounds and the cliff where we have our placement battles.

Placement battles are where a wolf of lower-ranking challenges a wolf of a higher ranking for their rank. If the lower-wolf successfully and fairly gets the higher-ranked wolf to submit, then they're promoted to that rank and the other wolf is demoted to the old rank. Sometimes, however, fights, especially for alpha or luna positions, can lead to death through the wolves killing one another or one of them falling off the cliff, instantly dying either from the rocks or the strong current that carries you for miles.

His office had polished oak floors and walls that hold portraits of older alphas and lunas alongside their families. He has a dark brown oak tree desk with lots of secret compartments and holes along with drawers. His desk is empty but of paperwork and a few pens or high lighters.

"Sit. Both of you." Still using his alpha voice, we immediately sit down for if we were to attempt to fight it, then it can lead to our bodies automagically and forcibly making us do what he told us to do.

"Now." He stopped using his alpha voice. For now. "What happened between you two? Others told me they saw Marshall exit the bathroom and Grant going in soon after. After that, complete chaos. Do you have any idea how embarrassing that is?!" We both immediately flinched at his sudden anger but continued to sit straight, trying to keep any dignity we still had.

"Having to hear from one of my wolf's that two of my sons were fighting on the training bathroom floor for who knows why! Not to mention that neither one of you probably thought of just challenging the other on the placement field!"

"Father-Shut it, Grant! I don't want to hear a single word from either one of you two! Wait for Luna to get here and then we'll decide what is to be done with the two of you!"

Eventually, we hear the door open and know it's Mother as she's the only one who's daring enough to open the door without knocking or asking permission to answer. She's also the only one to have gotten away with it.

I remembered when Marshall dared me to go open Father's office door for having gotten him in trouble earlier. Not wanting to appear weak, I did it without a second thought. Father was working on some paperwork when I randomly opened the door. He was already tired and frustrated because of a rogue problem we were having and he was having to send out alerts and answer emails from other alphas as we are the government pack of the United States.

I remembered the harsh glare he sent me and his demanding of why I had done that while he was busy. When I couldn't come up with an answer, he had gotten up and slapped me across the face, hard enough to bring tears into my eyes. I remembered him shouting at me that I was to listen to the rules and laws because they were placed down for a reason. I remembered him telling me to stop crying as alphas do not cry nor do they show any weakness.

Not even towards their children.

Too scared to disobey him even more, I quickly whipped away my tears and waited for Mother to come and get me. While she was taking me back to my and Marshal's room, she told me to never open Father's door for I will face his wrath like no other.

She told me a story about how once, while she was pregnant with me, she was sitting in the office room, waiting for him to be done with paperwork so they could sleep together, a traitor had swung the door open and aimed a gun at her. The traitor wanted the papers on the other United States packs to which my Father gave to them without a second thought for fear the traitor would shoot her.

He had to spend so much of his time rewriting those papers and getting the information from the packs once again. Having to face the alpha's anger and criticism while at it.

The traitor was never caught but is believed to be a dangerous rogue who somehow infiltrated the packhouse without anyone's knowledge and somehow knew the entire layout of it as well.

"What is it alpha that you call me here for?" Mother says in her calm and cool voice. Neither one of us bothers to look at her and simply stare straight ahead at Father, still not staring him directly in the eye.

"Luna. It appears that our two sons have decided to fight in the training bathroom for no reason it appears."

"Violence never breaks out unless there's a reason. You just need to find that reason. Often that reason only comes out when one is alone. Grant. Come with me. Grimsley. You stay and talk with alpha. We shall see who is lying and who is being truthful through this." Without a second word or even waiting for a response from Father, Mother turns around and walks away.

Grant glides up and follows a few feet from Mother and out of the office, closing the door quietly behind him.

Grimsley

"Grimsley. We can do this the easy way or the hard way. I'm giving you a choice despite what you just did. So pick it now or I'm deciding," Father growled while flashing his yellow wolf eyes at me.

I did my best to not flinch or look away while he spoke to me, frantically trying to think of some excuse on why I and Grant acted the way we did. Ideas from him threatening my position to just admitting the truth about Accalia rang through my head like water down a waterfall. Down an endless abyss where it'll never be heard from again.

"I'd also mention that there was the spotting of a girl jumping off of the High School's roof and then shifting into a white wolf midair before running off and into this very forest. As you may know, we have no wolves matching her description nor do we have any records of anyone recently shifting into her colored wolf form," Father continued to talk.

"Not to mention that wolves have claimed to have seen you interacting with a girl matching the description of the girl who shifted midair. I dare say it's a coincidence that you were caught talking to a possible rogue and you and Grant suddenly fighting. But I and Wolfsbane have a feeling it's not."

Father's wolf is named Wolfsbane after the power plant that can immobilize a wolf from shifting into their wolf form and using their added abilities in human form. It's highly dangerous for werewolves as a big enough dose of it can easily kill a werewolf within seconds or if someone's wolf is immobilized for long enough, then the wolf can potentially die, tearing the werewolf's soul.

Never to be able to get it repaired.

A wolf tearing itself and having it be immobilized are two separate things that often get confused by those who aren't educated enough about the differences. Having a wolf tear itself away from you is just simply where the wolf breaks its mind and body away from you. You're still able to call out to the wolf and feel its presence inside of you. But you just can't hear its mind or use its abilities as much as you used to be able to. Or at least as easily. The wolf is still conscious and comes back whenever it wants.

Having it immobilized means having it unconscious and unable to respond to you completely. You feel as though your soul is being ripped apart because Wolfsbane is the only known way to rip a wolf from its human counterpart. With the wolf unconscious, you're a normal human as you can't call out to it or anything. If the wolf is kept unconscious long enough, eventually it'll die from starvation as wolves eat when you eat.

"So Grimsley. What do you want to say? Or should I try asking Zarik?" Father Growled, saying Zarik's name in his alpha voice.

Upon hearing Father's alpha voice, Zarik was forced to come back to me as denying him can mean he's challenging Wolfsbane or if he tries to resist it, then his body and mind will act upon Father's will and commands, not his own.

Alpha voice is a special ability that is given to alphas and lunas. It's given to them by Luna herself if she deems them worthy enough to lead a wolfpack.

With an alpha or luna voice, they control all of their wolves within the pack. Alpha and luna voices will not work on rogues or other wolfpack members as the voice is designed for the pack that the alpha and luna are ruling and them only.

The voice is a mix of both the human and wolf parts of the soul, making it stronger than a regular voice or a wolf's voice by itself. The voices force the wolves that they're targeted at to bend to the alpha's or luna's will, whether it's their choice or not. A wolf, if strong enough, can deny or challenge the voice which means it's challenging or questioning the alpha or luna which often leads to a fight for the alpha or luna rank. If a wolf attempts to fight it, then the power of the voice becomes stronger and they feel as though chains or someone else is making them do the bidding of the alpha or luna.

Doing my best to appear and sound monotone, I say "I do not know what you are hinting at alpha." Knowing better than to call him Father when he's interrogating me as it'll just make him angrier and think I'm disrespecting him or challenging him.

"Oh, really Grimsley? So if I get Zarik to talk, he'll say the same thing to me? Or will he speak differently?" Father growled while glaring into my eyes, his wolf eyes now fully showing and glowing.

Challenging me to oppose his statement.

Keeping my head held and not showing any weakness, I simply tell him yes.

"Hmm....before I do get Zarik to talk for me. I want to hear what you have to say. Will you be truthful or will you tell me lies? After all, wolves can't lie when their alpha is speaking to them." I felt Zarik get pulled by the chains towards me even more, almost to the surface as while it wasn't a command that was given, he still needs to show that he's listening.

Zarik's eyes flash to prove that he's listening and I involuntarily give a slight nod, knowing it's Zarik responding to Father's statement.

"Talk."

"Yes, I was talking to her the day she decided to jump and shift. However, she never mentioned anything about doing it. She just simply talked about what any other teenage girl talks about. Grades, their plans for the weekend, etc. I did not know she would do that until she did it. I did not know she was a rogue, but simply a child someone had with a human and they didn't think she was a werewolf. She could have turned 18 that day and at that exact time, her shifting started.

I and Grant were fighting over the rights of being alpha. He challenged me and instead of going to the cliff, he lunged at me right then and now. In the bathroom. Marshall was just a coincidence."

"Lies. You know exactly what happened and why it happened," hissed Zarik at me. I immediately knew that Wolfsbane was listening to what Zarik was saying as wolves cannot only listen to their human counterparts talk but also the wolf counterparts, almost as if they were just background characters.

"Wolfsbane tells me differently. Grimsley. Since I feel generous today," said Father. "And don't take this as a sign of favoritism or anything. I'll give you one more chance. Tell me the truth and maybe I won't punish you. Lie to me again and I can't promise you won't be able to do any regular activities without feeling sharp pain for a few days. Maybe even weeks depending on how well the medics can take care of you." Father says in a deadly, but a monotone voice, not faltering in any way.

Not sure what to say, as I already knew I was caught, but I didn't want to straight-up admit that a no one who was never even looked at, nonetheless acknowledged or noticed was my mate and that I rejected it.

"Hmm. I see you rather let Zarik talk. Fine." Father growled. Father suddenly stood up so fast that his chair tipped over and fell over. He slammed his hands onto his desk, shaking it to the point that papers fell off and a small container containing pens and highlighters, fell to the ground, scattering its contents everywhere.

I nervously looked up and into Father's eyes, knowing what's about to happen now.

"You deserve this," growled Zarik so close in my mind it was as if he was standing right beside me and growling straight into my ear.

"Zarik. What happened on the day that that rogue jumped off the school and shifted midair? Does this have to do with Grimsley's and Grant's fight? Or any other of my sons?" Father said in his alpha voice.

I felt Zarik voluntarily take control to answer Father's questions truthfully.

"He's going to enjoy this," I thought dreadfully.

"That girl, who's name is Accalia Lupus, is our mate. Grimsley rejected her because he believed she was too weak to rule a pack and because he was embarrassed to have her as his mate. Thus, leading her to decide to attempt suicide. Her wolf, Orchid, took control midair and made her shift, having her run into the forest.

Soon after, Grimsley went off to skip school and went out with her sister, Chloe who he hopes is a werewolf and will reject her mate for him so that way he has a strong luna and someone who's far more popular than Accalia. I had torn myself away from Grimsley that night because Orchid had come to tell me that she rejects me as her mate and that she and Accalia are leaving the next day. Marshal was there that night, but we did not tell him anything. In the training bathroom, he threatened to tell you alpha if you started asking why I was absent from Grimsley and that's when Grant

pressed on. He asked about Accalia and that's when we got into a fight."
Zarik then let me have control again as he said what was needed to be said.

Grimsley

<hr>

For once in my life, I saw Father in shock and utterly speechless. He usually always has something to say or do after being confronted about something.

I felt the same knives and needles dig into my skin as Zarik once again tore himself away from me after Wolfsbane had talked to him. Not wanting to talk to me any more than he already had.

He finally seemed to have recovered from his shock because I found myself being yelled at by not only him but also Wolfsbane.

"I RAISED YOU FROM WHEN YOU WERE JUST A SECOND OLD! WHEN DID I EVER MAKE IT CLEAR THAT YOU COULD REJECT YOUR MATE SIMPLY BECAUSE THEY WEREN'T WHO YOU WANTED THEM TO BE?!" The entire office shook from the power of his voice and a few portraits even fell off the walls and landed with glass shattering and scattering everywhere as if there were an earthquake.

"I-I-You've always told me to show no weakness and to not allow anyone to get under my skin," I shuddered at first, trying to gain control of my voice and sound more steady than I felt. I was so scared of my Father, that I didn't feel Zarik come back due to hearing his alpha's voice raging at us and I felt him, coward, under Wolfsbane power and immediately submitted to him.

"BUT I NEVER SAID ANYTHING ABOUT REJECTING YOUR MATE! YOU'RE MATE IS WHAT COMPLETES YOUR SOUL! THEY'RE THE SOLE CREATURE THAT IS SUPPOSED TO RULE ALONGSIDE YOU! NO ONE ELSE!" I felt as though I were just a wolf pup and was seeing Death in the face as I wasn't supposed to be born because I wasn't the wolf's offspring.

If a male or female cheats on their mate, then the males will kill any offspring that isn't theirs without hesitation or a second thought while the females kill the mother, and if the pup or pups are born before she's dead, then the female will nurse and raise them as if they were her's. If the mother was killed while still carrying the pup or pups, then they will immediately die alongside the mother.

"Father, I-I-DO NOT SPEAK! AS OF NOW, YOU ARE NO SON OF MINE!" Father cuts me off as I attempt to defend my reason upon rejecting my mate. He was taking deep breaths, trying to calm down. I could see his eyes flashing between his usual blue and the yellow of Wolfsbane. Wolfsbane was trying to take control as I've never seen him this angry before. It almost looked as though Father wasn't fighting Wolfsbane as his eyes stayed a yellow color much longer than blue.

"Grimsley. This is an order rather than a request. I want you to go to Accalia's Lupus house and make it up to her. I don't care if you have to humiliate yourself in front of the entire pack or even give up your position as next-alpha, but you must make it up to her. Otherwise, I prevent you from becoming alpha." I felt Zarik's excitement at this order and it was obvious that he would wholeheartedly do it without a second thought.

"But Father, why must it matter if I do make it up to her? It's not a requirement to have your mate to become alpha." At my Father's furious glare, his eyes finally settling upon a glowing and fearful yellow, I instantly regretted what I just said. It was clear as crystal that Wolfsbane had just taken control of my Father and that furious couldn't even describe the glare he was giving.

"YOU'RE MATE IS A GIFT GIVEN FROM LUNA HERSELF! TO REJECT HER HER GIFT IS AN INSULT TO HER! SHE'S THE SOLE REASON WHY YOU'RE A WEREWOLF AND YOU SHOULD RESPECT HER AS YOUR GODDESS!" I visually flinched at Wolfsbane's rage and Zarik was now whimpering in horror, completely submitting to him and rolling over to expose his stomach to him as a sign of submission.

"YOU ARE TO GO TO HER HOUSE AND MAKE THINGS UP WITH HER! I DON'T CARE IF YOU HAVE TO GIVE UP YOUR RANK OR JUMP OFF A CLIFF! DO IT!" Wolfsbane commanded.

Zarik, upon hearing this command immediately jumped up and without me realizing it, had taken over and shifted right in Father's office.

"What are you doing?" I growled at him. "Why and how did you shift so fast?!"

"Shut up Grimsley. For once we're going to make things right, whether you like it or not," He quickly snapped before running out the office door and out the first open window he saw which thankfully was big enough for him to jump through with no issues.

Zarik never bothered to slow down for anything and when he was given weird looks or even asked what he was doing, he just simply ignored them all and kept running. Some wolves were able to feel his excitement and even tried running along, wondering what got him so excited as he's usually calm and monotone.

Everything was a blur for me as we ran through the forest and to the house we went to one night upon smelling our mate for the very first time. It looked the same as it was the last time. It was an old victorian home that looked like it would be abandoned as the wood was old and eroded at. The windows were kept clean and the lawn was freshly cut, that being the only indicator that people still lived in it. I saw a light glowing from one of the up floor windows and assumed it was Chloe as she had shown me her bedroom when we skipped class on the day that Accalia had jumped.

My heart fluttered a bit at the memory. How exotic it felt sneaking into her house while her parents were out doing something and we could easily be caught by either her parents walking in or the school calling my father and him tracking me down. I then thought back to how when we first kissed, I immediately pulled away. Something about it just felt off, like I shouldn't be there. The feeling of rebelling suddenly disappeared and was replaced with dread and even disgust. Without another word, I left Chloe's room and ran through the forest, avoiding the lake.

"Keep dreaming boy. For as soon as we enter that door, Chloe will only be a haunting memory and nothing more," growled Zarik which brought me out of my memory.

"Why do you hate her so much? She isn't that bad. She's better looking than Accalia at least. And more dominate...I think," I said.

"Keep telling yourself that for soon, Accalia will be the only girl that you ever look at or even touch," growled Zarik.

"How are you even going to knock on the door? You can't shift back because we'll be completely naked and I don't feel like having an angry wolf snapping at us."

"Like this." Zarik suddenly threw his shoulder into the door which quickly flung open, banging into the wall against it before attempting to close again only to be blocked by Zarik as he looked around.

Accalia's parents, Carly and John both stared at us in complete shock and horror. I could feel Carly's wolf, Flower whimper, and quickly submit to Zarik as he growls at her.

"Who the hell are you?!" Screamed John as he was now recovering from his shock and now just looked angry.

"John, that's Grimsley. The alpha's oldest son. Next in line for the alpha position. He must be here for Chloe. He must have smelled her," I heard Carly whisper to her husband in an excited but hushed tone as to not get Zarik anymore crazy as he already was.

John's angry expression suddenly turns into one of complete joy and excitement as he quickly gets out of the way of the stairs which I already knew led up to the bedrooms.

Without even a word, Zarik leaped up the stairs, two at a time and without any hesitation, ran towards Accalia's room.

I heard thumping from behind us and figured it was John and Carly following close behind. Accalia's door was closed and looked to be the most beaten up and less cared for as the paint was peeling off in huge chunks and the knob was eroded to the point it looked as though one hard hit could knock it off the door entirely.

Zarik slammed his shoulder into her door and the door also slammed into the wall and attempted to slam back into place but was stopped by Zarik.

Accalia's room looked like it had seen better days. It was painted a white color that was peeling off and looked as though water had hit it and was never cleaned off, making it a brownish color. She almost barely had anything in her room except a small white desk with paint peeling off and a white orchid with wilted flowers sitting in the center. The orchid looked almost dead as only a few of its leaves were still full and fresh and the others were all brown and shriveled.

There was a small bed against the nearest wall with the sheets cleaned off and made and what appeared to be a worn white wolf with silver eyes sitting upon it. Opposite the bed was another door open with clothes spilling out of it, whether they were dirty or clean, I could not tell.

There was a window letting in sunlight which shined directly onto the orchid and in front of the orchid, I saw a piece of paper.

"What? But this is what's her name room. Chloe's room is at the end of the hall. Why would you come here?!" John suddenly sounded angry again as he stared at Accalia's room and then Zarik.

Zarik let out a low growl and stalked slowly towards him, daring him to object again. John slowly backed away, his hands held in front of him in surrender as Zarik stalked closer and closer to him. His back hit the bed and he fell onto it, making the white wolf jump a bit and a piece of paper alongside it.

The paper landed neatly on top of the white wolf's head and covered its silver eyes.

Zarik smelled Accalia's scent on it and attempted grabbing it with his mouth gently. Because he was in wolf form, he couldn't read it so he shifted back into our human form. Carly, upon realizing this quickly ran out the room and moments later, came back with a big t-shirt and threw it at Zarik just as we were finally done shifting.

Quickly throwing it on, Zarik grabbed the note from my mouth and read it.

"Dear Grimsley,

I. Accalia Lupus. Accept you. Grimsley Canis. As my rejected mate."

Grimsley

After reading those words, it felt as though nothing in the world mattered anymore. Zarik howled out his pain and sorrow to the world, others responding to his howls as if their response could bring back what we just lost. I heard voices around me, but I couldn't make out what they were saying. Everything was blurry for me. The only thing that I could see was the note that Accalia had written for me. I wanted to just shift into my wolf and allow Zarik to engulf me, allowing him to decide what to do with ourselves.

I looked over at the white wolf stuffed animal and realized how it closely resembled Accalia in her wolf form. While the wolf had pure white fur and she had silvery-white fur, the eyes and almost everything else almost appeared to match one another. I gently lifted the stuffed animal by its back and upon getting a closer look at it, I saw there were stitches all around its neck, almost as if it had been torn off and then stitched together again. The fur was very coarse from the number of years it has taken. Yet it felt as soft as velvet at the same time. The eyes were made of the cheap plastic that stuffed animal companies use and the silver stayed strong in it.

I almost felt as though I were staring at Accalia's wolf eyes, as I've only seen a glimpse of them when she was in mid-shift. Zarik whimpered upon looking at the white wolf, saying it reminded him of Orchid and how Orchid had the most beautiful silver eyes he had ever seen.

I turned around to look at the wilted orchid. Now realizing how it represented Accalia. How Accalia went through so many hardships but still stayed strong. How she managed to stay beautiful and healthy despite the world being against her. But now her strength is deteriorating. And I'm the reason for it.

I look down at the white wolf and take a sniff at it. I could smell all the emotions that she had thrown onto it. Anger. Sadness. Sorrow. Rejection. I finally looked up at her parents to see that they were reading the note that was in front of the Orchid. Carly had tears in her eyes while John just looked sorrowful and troubled.

"I-I should have listened to Flower. She always knew what's best," sobbed Carly as John held her tightly. "She tried telling me to communicate with her. That she could sense Accalia's potential. But I never listened." Zarik's sorrow suddenly turned into anger so strong that I felt as though a gust of freezing wind just hit me from the inside and burst throughout my body. I had to grip the desk and take deep breaths to keep Zarik under control before he went on a rampage, most likely to tear Accalia's parents to shreds. Accalia. That single name almost seemed like a fire. A fire that burned through the ice and straight to Zarik. Zarik suddenly had a second of calmness before it was frozen over once again.

Quickly grasping onto the thought of Accalia, I started thinking about her. I've seen her in the halls before, always keeping her head down. Her long dark brown, sometimes even auburn depending on the light always being kept down and fell down her body in beautiful wavy hair that never seemed to be cut or even brushed at times. Her beautiful pale skin made it look like she rarely went outside despite the fact I always see her sitting by a window or sitting on the bleachers during one of my practices.

Despite how many times I see her in the halls or even classroom, I never seem to be able to see her eyes. Or at least what's hidden behind them. I've awkwardly made eye contact with her before, but she always turns her head away before I can fully understand the color of her eyes.

Sometimes I found myself laying in bed, wondering what color they would be and how they would look on her. I always found myself settling on a soft golden brown and before I can wonder why I've decided that, I would be in a deep sleep.

She always had a small petite figure, but she wore sweatshirts or loose clothing so I could never tell what she truly has. I easily towered over her as I'm 6'0" and she's 5'2". The closest we've ever been was when she had run into me that day. That day.

Upon remembering that day, Zarik suddenly remembered that I was the reason for her accepting our rejection. My rejection and leaving us heartbroken. Us.

I just thought that without realizing it or what it even meant. I knew it meant that I was even heartbroken over Accalia's sudden disappearance. How I also now blame myself for causing all this. How I regret everything that I did that day.

"This is all your fault! It's your fault that our daughter is now missing! What are you going to tell the police?!" John's angry voice breaks me out of my thoughts and I feel Zarik fighting me for control. I don't hesitate to let him.

"Listen here human," Zarik's voice was surprisingly calm, but venomous at the same time. "You can't even remember her name. What's that to say about you? Not a very good father huh?" I could feel John tremble underneath Zarik's sudden authority and showing, knowing my eyes have now switched over to Zarik's glowing amber eyes that felt as though they were piercing right through your soul.

"You-you don't know anything about my daughter or how I raised her!" He attempted to shout. He trembled, even more, when he saw Carly's heavily shaking form at Zarik's presence as she could feel his authority and power and Flower was retreating from it.

"At least I remembered her name. A father should always remember his children's names. Alpha had four children, including us and he never forgot our names or mixed us up. He always said that a good father remembers who his children are and what they do. I wonder what kind of father you are then," Zarik's voice has turned to an icy froth breath that could easily freeze anyone or anything in his path.

"Will then your father is a lair! No father can never mix up his children or even forget them! All fathers are-ack!" Within a few seconds, Zarik had shoved John up against the wall by his throat and was holding him as high as his arm could go.

"Don't you ever say that about alpha. You know nothing!" Zarik was now using his alpha voice and while sounding scarily calm, ice and venom dripped at every word he said. "You have no honor! You're a snake of a man! Give me one reason why I don't kill you here and now!" He snapped with ice and venom.

John could only sputter and choke as Zarik was seconds from crushing his trachea. Carly was pulling and begging at Zarik's arm to let John go or to at least release some of the pressure from his throat so he could breathe. He was starting to turn purple and was making weak attempts at kicking or grasping onto Zarik's arm.

"Zarik. Stop. You're taking this too far!" I finally shouted at Zarik, realizing that he fully planned on killing John and making it as long and torturous as possible.

"Think about Accalia! Orchid! How destroyed they'll be if they find out that you killed their father!" I started to attempt to fight Zarik for control but he was too strong. He was using all his built-up anger and sorrow to not only keep me on the sidelines but also take someone's life. John looked like he was about to past out from Zarik's grip when we all suddenly heard a scream.

We turned around to see Chloe holding hands with another werewolf which we quickly recognized as Skye, the Delta's son. Both looked horrified at the sight that beheld them. Chloe's from the state of her father and Skye from seeing Zarik in full control and remembering that I had went out with Chloe. Making him believe that she's my mate.

Zarik grinned at that thought and finally released John, not bothering to break his fall or make it any less painful as he drops directly onto the floor and into the arms of his worried wife who immediately starts asking if he's okay.

"Nice seeing you here Skye," Zarik says in a playful, but deadly voice. It was clear that Zarik fully intends on playing with Skye's emotions as a way to get him to stop doing what he's about to do.

"Z-Z-Zarik...what are you doing here?" Stumbled Skye as he backed away from Zarik, clearly hoping to make a run for it soon.

"'I'm here to see my mate. What else?" Said Zarik with a casual shrug of his shoulders as he circled Skye.

"Of-of course. I was just....uhh...taking her home! That's all! I promise!" Stuttered Skye, completely trapped by Zarik and unable to move.

"How funny. Do you think that little human is my mate? I hate to break your hopes. Or maybe it's not your hope, but she isn't my mate," Zarik said the last bit in a growl as a way to remind me of what I did and how because of it, we're in this position.

"Wh-what?!" Skye said in a completely shocked voice as he was now staring at Zarik directly in complete shock and confusion.

"You see. My human made a horrible mistake. Or should I even call it a mistake? Rather, a regretful decision in rejecting his mate and choosing her whore of a sister over what should have been rightfully mine from the very beginning. Because of this, she appeared to have left. Leaving us heartbroken," Zarik was now full-on growling, whether it was directed at me or Skye, I couldn't tell.

"Skye. You're the Deltas son, right? The next in line Delta at that even."

"Yes sir."

"Good. As your first duty as of being a Delta for me is to run to the packhouse. Tell anyone you can find about the horrid mistake my human had made and tell Alpha the entire story."

Just as he was about to go running out of the house, Zarik yelled for him to stop. Grabbing the two notes that were now laying on the bed, he handed them to Skye and told them to hand them to Alpha.

Skye just simply nodded and sprinted out of the house before Zarik could say anything else to him. Turning around to face the rest of Accalia's family he turned his gaze on every single one of them, giving Chloe a lingering hateful look.

"I want all of you to go to the packhouse. Tell the patrolling group that you were sent by me and to be taken immediately into the dungeons. All of you." Said Zarik using his alpha voice. Since Carly was a werewolf, her immediate response was to grasp John and Chloe and practically drag them out of the house and off into the woods where the packhouse will be.

Chloe protested the entire time and attempted to fight her mother off, but her mother almost appeared to be in a trance as she ignored her daughter's protests and continued towards the forest.

Now that we were finally alone, Zarik walked over to the bed and sat down on it. He gently picked up the white wolf and stared at it, stroking the fur on it lovingly. He looked up and looked around Accalia's room. She had nothing hanging on her walls and the only furniture in her room aside from the bed and desk was a small dresser with a single brush that looked as though it has never been used before.

"I'll have some wolves take her clothes and personal belongings to the packhouse and put them into my room. I'll take the orchid and wolf with me," muttered Zarik to himself.

Looking down at the wolf and then up at the orchid he allowed one single tear to drop down and hit the white wolf straight on its eyes. The tear glided across the eye and was soaked into the fur immediately as Zarik stood up to take the orchid as gently as he could and looked out Accalia's window.

We could see one of the many entrances to the forest in her backyard and thought back to the day when we went out on a run and ran up to the house, looking up at her window.

"Accalia. Orchid. Wherever you are. I promise to bring you back. I promise to make it all up and to love you until the end of time." Both me and Zarik said at the same time as a soft wind blew through the trees, making them rustle and drop more leaves.

Orchid

Water.

That's all that was running through my mind.

Ever since Accalia gave me full control, it has been non stopped moving. We avoided Zarik's pack like they were the plague. I barely knew the forest and Accalia has never gone this deep, we constantly were getting lost and twice now, we've nearly been caught by a patrol.

Because the river runs through the territory, we've been having to rely on ocean water, which only made us sick and more lethargic, thus leading to us barely being able to hunt or find shelter for us when it gets colder in the night.

Winter is coming. I could feel it. The leaves were all gone from the trees, turning into mush and mixing in with the soil. The days are shorter and heavy clouds constantly taunt us as they block out the sun and threaten to pour their icy water upon us. I could feel Accalia weakening as her body wasn't built to survive this type of climate like mine. I needed to find water. And fast.

I was about ready to just say "screw it" and go into the territory to get some water, not caring about the consequences. If a patrol group caught us and took us to the alpha, then I'll deal with the consequences. After all, nothing can be worse than having to reject my mate.

Remembering Zarik brought up a whole other type of pain through me as I remembered Zarik's face when I told him about what I and Accalia were planning on doing. Having to write out that note just made it all the worse as I knew that if Accalia accepts the rejection, then we would be completely torn from Zarik and Grimsley, not even the mating process will be able to tie us back together.

The only thing that could is death. Feeling weaker than ever, I finally collapsed onto the cold, hard ground and let out a heavy sigh, finally feeling all my strength leaving me.

"Orchid? Are you okay?" I heard Accalia ask me, concerned.

"I'm sorry Accalia. I don't think I'll be able to take us any farther. This entire forest is overruled by elite packs, so no matter where we go, we'll never be safe. Besides, your parents will soon realize you're gone right? Or at least Flower will take control and make your mother look for us." I suggested. I knew Accalia's response before she even did it.

She got quiet. It wasn't like she was pulling away from me or blocking me out. She was just thinking. Thinking about everything that I and her have just gone through and if it's worth leaving.

"We've already gone this far. Grimsley nor Zarik will welcome us with open arms. My parents probably haven't even noticed that we're gone and everyone's living out their normal lives as if we never existed. Orchid. I don't care where we go. As long as we're together, I don't care. You're the only thing at this point that's keeping me going." I could tell Accalia was about ready to burst into tears, and I felt as though I were about to do the same thing.

"I know they won't. And I know everyone probably doesn't even realize that we're gone. I want to keep us safe. But I can't as long as we're in this state. We need to find a new state to live in. One where no one will recognize us or even know our past.

But I don't know where we would go for that. Nowhere is safe for us. We're rogues. We're unwanteds. Wolves don't want to notice us for a whole separate reason. One that is more violent than not wanting a mate."

"Orchid. We need to risk it and go into the territory. I don't care about which territory. As long as it has water and some sort of shelter that we can use. But we can't die now. Not with how far we've been able to come."

"Alright. Hopefully, snow will fall soon so then our scent will be masked and we'll be able to blend in better."

With that being said, I took a deep breath and got back up on my paws. As sick as I was, I was still able to hear water running, despite the coldness that is engulfing it slowly. Shakingly, I headed towards it, straining my ears for any sounds of pawsteps beating at the ground like drums.

For elite packs, they don't bother with hiding their pawsteps. I could hear them before I felt their thunderous steps as they picked up dirt and debris as they ran, letting the entire forest know that they're there and that they're dangerous.

Exactly what they want. They dare rogues to try and tread on their land. Their pawsteps are just symbols of their power and strength. Mocking rogues. Mocking them by reminding them that they have no one. That they have no pack to love and be loved back. That they're unwanted. That death is the only thing that wants them.

I let out a low growl at this thought. I and Accalia aren't savages. We're not barbarians. We're not rejects either. We're simply nothing. We have no meaning in this world. But we continue to fight. At that thought, I felt a sudden surge of strength and speed. I ran faster than I've ever run. The entire forest was a blur of mixed colors as my paws stomped on the ground as if I were a cold-blooded beast.

No. That isn't the right word for us. Inferno. That's what I and Accalia are. We're an inferno that should not be tested. We feed off the false names that we're labeled with and only the truth can extinguish us. We're a walking blaze that no one knows about. Just like turning on your stove or oven. You don't acknowledge it after you're done with it. Because of that simple mistake, we can easily burn you to a crisp.

~

We finally reached a river that didn't appear to be guarded and no scent of wolves was around it. I drank hungrily at the icy water, not noticing the piercing ice spears that slid down my throat like silk. I almost stopped breathing from the amount of water that I was drinking as I had to remind myself that even infernos need air to survive.

Once I and Accalia finally felt refreshed, I looked up to scan our surroundings. I couldn't hear nor see any other wolves and the scents around the river are stale. I walked around the border of the river for a bit, looking at where it led when I suddenly heard it.

Pawsteps.

I cursed at myself for being so careless and not immediately running for it after we got our drink. Thinking fast, I quickly sprinted towards the way we came, hoping they wouldn't be able to catch up to us.

The sudden sound of pawsteps surrounded us and I realized we had no choice. Even if we made it back to the border, they wouldn't stop chasing us until we surrendered or fought them. I quickly made a U-turn to face our pursuers and saw two wolves sprinting towards us, showing no sign of stopping. I heard a growl behind us and knew that now is too late to attempt to run.

Letting out a growl of my own, I let out a warning bark, warning them not to come any closer. The smaller one stopped momentarily before slowing down to a stalk and growling lowly. The bigger one started to do the same and when I felt the wolf behind us move in closer, I quickly turned around and snapped my jaws at it as a warning. It flinched away from my fangs but quickly started stalking closer.

"Don't bother fighting. You're outnumbered. Might as well surrender now and face the consequences," said the bigger wolf.

"A step closer and I won't hesitate to rip your throat open," I growled back, locking eyes with him. He wasn't anything too special. Usual brown wolf with some black marking around his face and shoulders. The smaller one was a light grey with darker grey around his face and shoulders along with some white blended in.

"She's tough. That's new for a female rogue. Usually, the females roll over as soon as they're caught," said the wolf behind me. I noticed it was a female from the tone of her voice and she sounded bored as ever.

"There are always exceptions. Why are you here rogue? Don't you know this is the Tourmaline Pack? The top elite and an alpha pack of all Northern American packs?" Said the bigger one.

"I'm simply crossing. I needed a drink of water. I'll be gone and out of your sight if you let me go," I said as calmly as I could.

The two wolves laughed as if I said something funny before the smaller one spoke up.

"Hey, she kinda reminds me of the wolf that Grimsley's looking for."

At the mention of our ex-mate, my heart immediately stopped. Grimsley was looking for us?! What about Zarik?! Why were they looking for us? Did they realize that they missed us or did their alpha make them? I let out a low growl at the thought. If Grimsley was looking for us simply because his father ordered it, then I am not going back.

"I think she is. He wasn't very descriptive with her appearance. All white with silver eyes. She matches. But then again, any other wolf could too," said the female.

"What's your name wolf?" Asked the bigger one.

"Orchid. Why does it matter to you? I'm just some rogue that won't matter to you once you kill me," I growled, daring him to argue.

"That's the name that Zarik gave us. I think she is Grimsley's mate. Why are you running away from him? Any other female would have been thrilled to have him as a mate," said the bigger male.

I just glared at him, refusing to give him the answer.

"He rejected you, didn't he?" The smaller one asked.

I looked at him shocked. How did he know that?! Did Grimsley tell him? Did he find out through someone else?

"I'm Valentine. I'm Grimsley's youngest brother. That's how I know. Also, Zarik ordered that everyone in the pack know as a way to humiliate Grimsley," explained the smallest one.

"I don't blame her for running then. If my mate rejected me, I would want to run too," said the female.

"I didn't reject you, so don't talk like that," said the bigger male.

"Anyways, I'm sorry Orchid. Truly. If it were up to me, I would let you run. Even help you. But I was given orders. I'm afraid you're going to have to come with us," said the female.

"I'm not going anywhere near that wolf!" I barked, anger suddenly taking over me.

"Orchid. Listen. I know my brother can be a complete jerk sometimes. Or actually, all the time. But he truly misses you. He hardly eats, sleeps, bathes, anything. He won't even snap at me or Grant when we try to purposely annoy him. He won't even fight Marshall when Marshall challenges him. Please Orchid. Come with us. I promise it'll be worth it."

I looked into Valentine's eyes and could tell he was being honest. He wasn't lying about how Grimsley was handling our disappearance. For once we were noticed. But do we want to be noticed?

That sudden thought came to me before I was about to agree. Do we truly want to be noticed? Do we truly want to go back to Grimsley, knowing that even if we do, there's no way we'll be able to retie the knot that held us together? Once a mate accepts the rejection and the wolf rejects the mate as well, there's no turning back.

We won't be able to live happily together, feeling as though something is missing. Eventually, that feeling will bring chaos between us and we won't be able to fix it. We'll both be even more hurt than we already are and there's no way we'll be able to fix it. Eventually one of us will give into the chaos and the other will no longer have control of their emotions.

They'll go on a mad rampage, destroying everything within their sight. Killing innocents, risking the exposure of us to humans, hurting themselves even more as they slowly die a painful death. I sadly shook my head. I couldn't do that to either one of us. It won't be fair to either of us. As much as I hate the pain that we're in right now, I couldn't bear any more of it.

"I'm sorry. Accalia accepted his rejection and I rejected Zarik. There's nothing we'll be able to do. Tell Grimsley to move on. Try to love another and forget about us. He'll be happier and safer that way," I tell Valentine.

"I know. But there has to be a way to be able to get you two tied together again. Mother knows all sorts of old traditions and ceremonies. She's bound to know something! Just, please. Come with us. I can't bear seeing Grimsley like this any longer. It'll break his heart even more if he finds out we found you but you escaped," begged Valentine.

"I'm sorry. I've made up my mind. I'm sure your mother would have been able to do something, but in case she can't, I don't want to risk it."

"Then we'll take you by force," said the bigger one.

I got into a defensive position as he stalked towards me when suddenly the female jumped in his way.

"Wait! He'll be even more upset if we bring her harm." Turning around to face me she gave me an apologetic look.

"What? What are you-" I was cut off when she suddenly pressed her paw against my nose and when I breathed in, I smelled some sort of strong herb or medicine.

That's when everything went dark.

Orchid

I groggily opened my eyes, immediately analyzing my surroundings once I remembered what just happened. We appeared to be in some sort of dungeon or cave even as the walls were pitched black and absorbed all light that was emitted from the few torches hanging on the walls. There was a small hole in the ground in a corner which I assumed was a bathroom and in the distance, I could hear running water.

"Says he misses us and then throws us in a dungeon," I thought bitterly as I looked for a way out.

"Orchid. Where are we?" Asked Accalia.

"Some sort of cave or dungeon. The patrol must have brought us here once we were knocked unconscious," I explained.

"Do you remember anything? All I remember is that wolf pressing her paw against your nose and suddenly everything went dark and quiet."

"I'm afraid that's all I remember too. We must be in the Tourmaline pack's territory as I highly doubt they would have brought us anywhere else but to their territory."

"Have you been able to find a way out?"

"No sadly. I just woke up as well. I don't think there is any way out unless we got a guide or something." The sound of footsteps broke our conversation and I quickly looked into the darkness. Despite my strengthened eyes, I couldn't see anything and it wasn't until the silhouette of a boy appeared that I could see who it was.

"Valentine," I said, automatically realizing who it was based on the small amount of power he gave off.

"I'm sorry about having to throw you into the dungeons. It was just too risky having you up here with the other pack members and Grimsley being in such a horrid state," he explained, sounding very apologetic.

"Why? And wouldn't you want me near him then?" I growled, not letting my guard down with him. I've let my guard down with him once, I wasn't about to do it again. Especially now that I'm in unknown territory.

"Because the members will growl at you and even try to attack you as they blame you for the state that Grimsley's in. He hasn't been the nicest or tolerable wolf around. Constantly snapping orders like he's the alpha only to have father snap at him and then give different orders, short-tempered, hostile towards anyone, restless, just in a horrible state of mind.

But because of those characteristics, I fear what he may try to do if he realizes that the tie between you two is no longer tied and there's nothing for him to do. He could become worse than he already is and give in to the chaos or he could make even more desperate attempts at figuring out how to retire the tie while also never letting you out of his sight. Almost as if you were a criminal and he was an officer."

I stared at Valentine with an emotionless expression, not wanting to give him any signs to feed off or give him an even more reason to keep us separated.

As much as I hate what he did to Accalia, I can't deny the feeling of longing and loneliness that I and Accalia have been feeling. We've been feeling lost and hopeless, constantly second-guessing ourselves and just wanting to return home.

But there is no true home for us.

We're nothing. We're the fire in the furnace. No one pays mind to us, believing that we won't someday grow stronger and that they'll never have to acknowledge us.

"Please understand you two. I and my brothers will visit every day with plenty of food and water to keep you alive and well-fed. This is a cave with many tunnels that only the elite members of the pack know their way through. You can explore them and we'll easily find you. But don't bother looking for an exit. There's none here. I can promise you that," Valentine's words broke me out of my thoughts and I looked back at him, daring him to keep going on.

Getting the message, he just simply nodded and walked off. Being engulfed by the darkness and his footsteps being embraced by nothingness.

"Accalia. Do you want to take control for a bit? I know you didn't want to take control any longer, but being cooped up like that can't be good for you," I said to Accalia.

"How? You were almost always cooped up like me and you never complained."

"That's different." I sighed. "You shifting into your wolf form is also my form. While we do share the same two bodies, just like conjoined twins with heads on the neck, I have superior control over the wolf form while you have superior control over the human form. Eventually, your body will become weak and more sensible the less you just do it. Just like the wolf form."

I could tell Accalia was debating on it as we laid in silent, waiting for what her next decision or move would be.

"Fine." She finally said. "I'll do it. But as soon as we hear something, you're taking over again."

I felt our bones crack and shift around as we shifted back into human form.

It felt so weird being in control again. It wasn't until when I could barely stand did I realize how long I've been in wolf form and allowing Orchid control the entire time. It almost felt as though I were learning to walk again as I struggled to get strength back into my legs and remember how to use them.

I looked around the cave that we were in, there were torches lining the walls which led through different tunnels which I could only assume led to more tunnels. The walls were made of complete stone and dirt, proving that the cave was natural.

There was a pair of chains on the opposite wall that was getting rusted at. They appeared to have dug into the stone and dirt but didn't appear to be able to stop anyone as the chains appeared delicate and could easily snap within one hard tug.

"Not careful about keeping prisoners huh?" I thought.

"Those aren't regular chains. They're made of wolfsbane. Wolfsbane is the only known thing that is able to weaken a wolf to the point of death.. It makes it so the human doesn't have any abilities that the wolf gives them, such as faster healing and speed. You're basically a regular human while your wolf is at the brink of death," said Orchid.

I stared in horror at the chains, now knowing what they're truly able to do and what that would mean for me if I was to be put in those. Ever since having Orchid around, I can't think of a life without her. With

Grimsley rejecting me and my family not caring about me, life almost seems meaningless.

Almost.

Orchid is truly the only thing that is keeping me alive and stopping me from deciding to just give up and allow myself to get swallowed by the trees and earth. Living without her would be like living without happiness. I would just be an empty void with nothing to do in my life and no one to care about or to be cared for by.

"Accalia. I hear someone coming. And you're not gonna like who it is," Orchid suddenly breaks me from my thoughts and I ask her who it is and why.

"It's Grimsley. And I think you know why."

Grimsley

"She's here. I can smell her." Zarik kept repeating those words to me until finally, we were stomping down the stairs that lead into the cave.

Ever since finding out about Accalia's disappearance, Zarik refuses to let me take control for more than five minutes. It's been constant demands for wolves to search harder and to double-check places they've already checked.

I could tell the wolves were growing tired of Zarik's constant demands and refusal of giving up and ending the search. But none of them had the nerve to straight up say that to Zarik for word of what he did to Skye quickly spread which meant fear for Zarik's wrath spread as well.

I couldn't tell if it was Father's command or Zarik's own free-will that he was acting like this for I've never seen him like this. He was always calm and honest about his thoughts. He rarely snapped and when he did, he would often close himself out right after, leaving the receiver more guilty than fearful.

Once at the bottom, I could tell someone was here as the torches had been lit up and I could faintly smell something different. Something intoxicating.

Zarik could clearly tell what I was thinking because I could hear him smirk, knowing full well that he wouldn't let me live this down and that he will bring it up every waking moment for me. I was about to say something in an argument when we suddenly heard soft footsteps hit the hard stone. I and Zarik both perked up at that sound. While Accalia's family was placed in an elite cell she was placed in the normal dungeon. Where we keep all the other prisoners.

At this thought I raced down the stairs, taking two at a time. The bottom seemed so far and every two steps I take it keeps getting farther and farther away. Eventually I grow annoyed with this and shift into Zarik so I can jump down to the bottom. I see the chains hanging on the walls, indicating we either did not have any prisoners or someone let them loose.

"Someone let them loose." I growled to which Zarik let out a huff of rage as we quickly followed Accalia's scent along with the scent of the prisoners. We run down tunnel after tunnel, Accalia's scent getting stronger as we run; but so do the prisoners' scents. We hear growls and whimpers coming a bit further down and we run even faster if that was even possible, worried that we would see the body of Accalia; not alive.

We turn a corner and see two of the prisoners stalking another wolf; that smells exactly like Accalia. They either don't realize our presence or choose to ignore us as their sole focus is on Accalia. I recgonize them as the rogues that we captured a few days ago, roaming the territory without a care. They would not tell us what pack they were from or where they came from, so we through them into the dungeon until we could further interrogate them. One was a red wolf and theo ther a black wolf. Both were twice Accalia's size and I could tell they were preparing to attack.

Accalia's eyes were the silvers of Orchid's eyes but I could see depression and hopeless in them. Orchid and Accalia were weak, they were in no form to fight the two males. Even if they were healthy they wouldn't be able to completely take them down, but they would of at least had a chance.

Orchid looked completely broken. Her fur was now a dirty grey, no longer the lustful and bright white that it was. The fur was thinning to show more skin and bone which made her look more like an abused wolf pup than a full-grown wolf. Her tail was between her legs and it looked more like bone than anything else. Seeing Orchid in that state, I could only imagine what Accalia looked like. She was already delicate and fragile looking before she left, now she probably looked like skin and bones and also completely broken.

I let out a growl which alerts the two wolves of my presence and they quickly turn around to face me. Their fur rises as it wasn't before and they begin stalking towards me. I stand my ground and growl at them even more, not taking my eyes off of them while I move. I circle them as they watch and I stop when I'm directly in front of Accalia and Orchid. I begin to pace back and forth, making sure to press Accalia and Orchid against the wall so then the males wouldn't stand a chance at getting to her without getting through me first.

One bares his teeth at me while the other stalks closer. I bare my teeth back and snap at the one stalking closer, the black one. The black one stops in his tracks and almost looks as if he were about to submit when he suddenly jumps and lungs for what's behind me; Accalia.

I quickly get on my hind legs and knock him back to the ground, making sure to pin him down there and snarl in his face. He quickly whimpers as I put more weight onto his body; telling him not to mess with me any further. Just as I'm about to snap his neck I hear Orchid let out a growl.

Suddenly I see Orchid meeting the red wolf mid-air and somehow managing to knock him over. My shock quickly turns into pride as I see that despite their state, they still have a inferno in them that shouldn't be handled carelessly. But Orchid isn't able to stay on top of him for very long. He quickly knocks her off of him and without thinking I jump in between them right as he goes in to bite her.

I feel teeth grab the tip of my right ear and break through the delicate cartilage there, ripping a piece of my ear off. I let out a howl of pain and blood is now pouring and covering my right eye, making it hard for me to see.

I hear Orchid shout my name and then a growl as she lunges at the male again. In my left eye I see the black wolf getting up and getting ready to tackle Accalia as she and the red male roll on the ground, snapping and clawing at each other. I knock him over with my shoulder into the wall to which I hear his skull make contact and I see he's unconscious.

I run over to Accalia and the brown wolf and without thinking, I grab the nape of whichever happened to be on top and pull them off. I see it's Orchid to which she quickly pulls away from me and is about ready to tackle the male when I quickly shove myself between her and him, seeing how he had already ripped pieces of her fur off and she was bleeding in multiple wounds. The wolf rises to his feet and smirks at us.

"What?" I growl at him, confused but also angry.

"We were just a pure distraction. For them. Remember Grimsley? There was five of us."

I hear Orchid whimper and when I turn around, I see three wolves come out of the shadows. We were cornered.

Grimsley

<hr>

While I might be able to take on two wolves, there's no way I could take on four all at once. This was a trap and I should have known. The rogues must have known about Accalia and how she is my mate, so they somehow got free of their chains and cornered her until I came so they could kill me. How they managed to get free remains a mystery to me.

"Such a shame we have to kill a pretty little wolf. She would have been fun to play with." The red one growls and stalks closer to us. One wolf was grey, another brown, and the last one grey. They were all caught walking together in the territory and surprisingly didn't give a fight. They allowed us to take them to the dungeon and even allowed us to shackle them.

I let out a growl at him and press myself closer to Accalia and Orchid, making sure that none of the rogues can get close to her without getting through me. Blood dries over my right eye, blocking part of my vision as all I can do is snap at any wolf that moves. They were taking their time; just like a cat and mouse. They were taking pleasure from our suffering; wanting it to last as long as possible.

I heard Orchid and Accalia growl behind me and nudge their way to my right; they weren't going down without a fight and they wanted it known.

I notice the rogues exchange glances at each other when she does this; almost as if they were debating on attacking or not still. That was the only hesitation I needed.

I lunge at the brown wolf, taking him completely by surprise and I sink my teeth into the soft fur and skin of his neck. He lets out a gasp of surprise before I feel his claws sink into the skin of my stomach and rip at it. I hear Orchid and Accalia scream my name before one of the other wolves jumps on her.

I release my grip on the brown wolf and snap my head around to see Accalia and Orchid being pressed to the ground as the red one presses down on her neck, keeping her still. As I make a step towards them I see the red wolf press even harder on Orchid's neck, making her let out a whimper.

"One more move wolf and I won't hesitate to snap her neck." The red wolf growls while staring me straight in the eye. While he is the smallest and skinniest of the group, he appears to be the smartest and most cunning. I don't take another step forward and I can feel all the other wolves' eyes on me. The blonde one finally came back to consciousness and started stalking us as well, making us cornered.

"What do you want?" I growl, keeping my eyes locked on the red wolf's body which is on Accalia and Orchid.

"It's not what we want, but what she wants." The red wolf growled.

"She?" I question, confused. Any wolf that goes rogue is immediately reported to all other packs in North America so we are aware of them and can track them down before they can harm anyone. But there has been no female reported going rogue; the only one that did go, rogue, was caught. So what other female rogue could they possibly be talking about?

"Exactly how do you plan on leaving though? You're in a dungeon with no exits and even if you do somehow leave, there's an entire pack outside waiting for you."

"We have our ways." Snarled the red wolf. "Grab him!" I felt all the rogues circle me and was getting ready for them to pounch on me when suddenly three of the four wolves were tackled. I look over and see a dark grey wolf, another brown wolf with lighter tips, and a blonde wolf. My brothers.

Marshall was the grey wolf, Grant being the brown wolf with lighter tips, and Valentine being the blonde wolf. Marshall was taking on the brown wolf, Grant the blonde one, and Valentine the black wolf. I tackle the grey wolf who was equally surprise by the sudden attack; but responded later than me. Growls and howls filled the room as I and my brothers fought the rogue wolves. I heard the brown wolf let out a cut scream of pain as Marshall bites his neck, killing him instantly.

Marshall lunged at the black wolf that Valentine was fighting since Valentine's wolf is smaller than average since he shifted early on in life. I quickly ended the grey wolf and started to frantically search for Accalia and Orchid along with the red wolf. I couldn't find them anywhere and I suddenly felt someone jump on top of me.

I looked and saw the blonde wolf digging his claws into my side and I attempted to shake him off. I felt Marshall shove him off of me and one look at Marshall and the blonde wolf told me that Marshall would be able handle the blonde wolf on his own. I went back to frantically searching for Accalia and Orchid. I found them still underneath the red wolf and Grant appeared to be stalking towards them.

I ran over and I saw Grant glance over at me. I thought I saw a look of shock on his face but it quickly disappeared and Grant lunged at the red wolf, knocking him off of Accalia and Orchid. Before I could reach them Grant ended his life with a swift bite to his neck.

Accalia

"Grimsley, you need to leave. I can't do anything with Zarik snapping at me whenever I even make a move towards Accalia."

"I have him under control, promise. We don't want to leave her side. Not after everything we just put her through."

"That's not the issue, Grimsley. The issue here is Zarik growling at Luca every time we try to touch even a inch of Accalia's skin. Don't make me have mother take you out of the room and sit in waiting room. I shouldn't have even let you in here since you aren't medically trained."

"C'mon Marshall. I'll get Zarik to calm down. Just let us stay here with her."

"Can't do Grimsley. Sorry. As soon as I'm done stitching her wounds I'll let you back in."

"But-no buts Grimlsey. You might be the alpha out in the battlefield but I'm the alpha in the hospital and unless Accalia personally asks for me to let you stay, than I have to ask you to leave so then I work on her in privacy."

"Marshall. She is my mate. I fucked up, I'll be fucking up again by leaving her side Now let me stay."

I let out a groan which causes both Grimsley and I'm assuming Marshall to turn around and look at me. I recgonize Marshall from the high school, while we never interacted he was one of the few people who would at least acknowledge me; even if it was just a smile. I've noticed how Marshall always seems to be with the science students or has his head buried in a book despite the amount of girls constantly trying to get his attention. During gym class I noticed he would hide out underneath the bleachers by himself and just watch the rest of the class; coach never seemed to care.

"Accalia...you're awake." I first hear Grimsley and turn around to look at him. His hair was a mess, falling in all different directions and some strands falling into his eyes, almost looking at though they were going to poke him in the eye. The second thing I notice is the teeth marks in his ear; the missing cartilage. The skin had grown back on it but now the tip of it was shredded and sharp looking; like a wolf ripped out his ear.

"Heh, ya...that. The rogue took a good piece out of Grimsley. But don't worry, he still has his hearing so he can't be excused for not listening." Marshall's higher-pitched voice cuts me out of my daze and I look over at him. He's wearing a doctor's coat and scrubs along with a stethoscope around his neck and a mask down on his chin.

"All of the rogues were taken care of; none of them can hurt you nor anyone else now."

"The red one...when he was holding me down, he kept talking about a woman...or maybe two women? Something about how they wanted me alive for testing and my blood. He also mentioned something about how he was from a pack?"

"A pack? Do you happen to remember the name?" Marshall asks.

"The nearest packs we have are the BloodMoon, Obsidian, and North-Wind packs. Any of them sound familiar?" Asks Grimsley.

"BloodMoon. He kept saying that word over and over again, something about how they'll regret it...whatever it is."

"That would make sense. The BloodMoon pack is known for having the most red wolves in any pack. Although I don't remember them mentioning any of their packmates going rogue," said Marshall.

"That wouldn't be the first time they don't don't alert us. They are known for keeping to themselves often and thinking they're better than us," said Grimsley. "Did he happen to mention a name? Did any of the rogues say a name or anything specific?"

"The red wolf mentioned a name. It sounded like a guy's name. Madrid? Maverick? Something like that." I said.

"Maddox?" Asks Marshall.

"Ya. He kept repeating that name, it sounded like Maddox did something to him because he did not like him. Kept talking about how he'll show him the end?" I said.

"Maddox is the beta of the BloodMoon pack. I know he has two other brothers; Dante and Denver. Did any of them call the red wolf that?" Asks Grimsley.

"The black wolf called him Dante. I remember he called the black wolf Jet, kept saying something about why he can see why his pack kicked him out?" I said, trying to recall any other names that were mentioned.

"The Obsidian pack did just banish one of them packmates. Jet Corvids. I heard they banished him for killing a human tourist over a gambling dispute. He apparently waited outside the building for the tourist to come out and ambushed him in wolf form. Alpha was having a nightmare trying to cover it up since his wife saw the entire thing happen," said Marshall.

"It would of made more since for them to prison him or send him to us instead of banishing him but that's a issue for another day." Grimsley turns over to look at me and I see a look in his eyes that I never saw in my parents' eyes even if I managed to make honor roll in high school every year; admiration. For a second I forget how to breath as I'm so used to stone looks and brief glances that barley survey any emotion. "What about any other details?"

"The blonde wolf was named Cello. The brown one was Devin and the grey one Grayson. They didn't mention their pack but it sounded like Devin and Grayson were family members of some kind. They seemed very close. The red one seemed to be the leader of them. The black one kep appearing to want to attack but he kept telling him to wait," I said.

"Cello doesn't surprise me. He's a well known rogue who is normally harmless; the worst he done is pee in front a bunch of pups while ranting about how the government is trying to silence him but they haven't been able to. He's old, but normally harmless. No one knows which pack he's from," said Marshall.

"Devin and Grayson...those names sound familiar but I don't know why," said Grimsley.

"Wasn't there a gay couple who left their pack because of the abuse they were facing from their packmates? Could that have been them?" Asked Marshall.

"Ya, I remember them. They were from the Cave pack. But last I heard the Fabled pack took them in and made one of them beta," said Grimsley.

"Could it be possible they were using fake names?" I asked.

"You aren't wrong. It wouldn't be the first time rogues went under fake names to throw us off. Devin and Grayson were already getting a bad reputation from their previous pack. It could be possible that those two are previous members of the Cave pack. Although the Cave pack is across the country, they have to be traveling for days to get here," said Grimsley.

"I don't remember the Cave pack reporting any rogues recently. Actually, I don't remember any reports of them at all recently," said Marshall.

"Reports?" I said.

"Every country has a royalty pack that the smaller packs have to report to. If they banish someone or someone decides to go rogue, they have to report it to their royal pack. If human lives are mixed in, such as a attack or marriage, the royal pack needs to be notified of that. Even vampire sightings need to be notified to the royal pack. Every year the royal packs gather for a meeting to discuss everything happening in their country. Sometimes smaller meetings are held among bordering packs if needed," explained Grimsley.

"The Cave pack not reporting back to us is suspicious. That could mean they are planning a rebel or something happened to them. It could have been a vampire attack as they are near major cities," said Marshall.

"That's a issue we'll discuss later. Right now we need to focus on you Accalia." Grimsley looks over at me and inspects the injuries I've endured. I surprisingly don't feel any pain but when I look down I see stitches along my arm; starting at my wrist and ending at my elbow.

"It's only temporary." Marshall breaks me out of my thoughts. "It's to help your body heal more cleanly and quickly. Us werewolves heal at a much faster rate than humans but that doesn't mean we are indestructible. A good example of that is Grimsley's ear."

"Why can't I hear Orchid?" I ask, now realizing she hasn't spoken since I've woken up.

"I gave you some anesthesia to help stitch you up and also so then you won't move around as much. The anesthesia tends to take a bit longer to wear off for our wolves. She should be waking up anytime now," explained Marshall. After that, Marshall got up and left the room, leaving I and Grimsley alone.

"Accalia...I know you probably don't want to see me right now and I don't blame you, but you're in serious danger as of right now. Those rogues knew who you are and somehow planned this attack on you. Your family is already here in a protected cell and you're allowed to visit them whenever you want. I can make arrangements for guards to be at your house if you like to stay there or you can stay here in the pack house." Grimsley sits down on the doctor's chair that Marshall was sitting on and comes closer to me, close enough for me to reach out if I wanted to.

"What's a pack house?" I asked, unsure if I wanted to stay here or not.

"It's where you are currently. All the pack members of a pack live in it. It's like a college dorm but with bigger rooms and space. We have separate buildings such as this one, the hospital wing, another one is where important meetings are held along with the Alpha's office, there's a gym where we train, it's like a college campus."

"If I stay here, I could be potentially attacked again and Valentine mentioned the members aren't happy with Grimsley which means they wouldn't be happy with me neither. If I go back home, I go back to all the memories of my childhood," I thought to myself.

"I know you don't like the circumstances, neither do I, but it might be best we stay at the pack house." Orchid's voice breaks me out of my thoughts.

"Orchid! You're back!"

"Yes, I am sorry Accalia. I thought I was taking us away from danger but I only brought us back to what we were running from."

"No, I'm the one who made that mistake. I thought running away from our problems would solve them but it only made them worst. All we did was hurt others."

"Accalia. You shouldn't be blaming yourself for what happened." Grimsley cuts me and Orchid off. "If anything I should be the one to blame. I thought I was doing you a favor by rejecting you and putting you in that bathroom like nothing happened. I thought you would just move on from me and leave town...unnoticed." Grimsley pauses after saying that, no longer looking me in the eye and now looking downcast.

"I know nothing I say or do can ever reverse the pain I put you through and I don't blame you for whatever you say or do to me. I don't blame you for not trusting me anymore. But I am not lying when I say this." Grimsley looks up and directly at me with a serious face, I've never seen him so serious before. "You are in danger and need to be protected. I or someone else can train you in self-defense and teach you how to combine your strength with Orchid's. But as of right now, we need you to be under protection. After this rogue issue is taken care of, you can skip town if you like. Hell I'll help you get away from me and this place completely. I'll give you money, transportation, anything you need to leave."

"The decision is yours," said Orchid.

"I'll stay here. I'll train with others." I said, having already made my decision.

Accalia

"You'll be training with Ember first. She is the best trainer for agility. You can train with her for a little bit and then I'll take you to Gunner, he's the weights trainer so he'll help you with building your strength." I and Grimsley were walking through several hallways, many of them with glass walls where I could see forest everywhere and wolves running around; some had kids riding on their back while others were dragging deer carcasses to what I assume is a slaughterhouse.

"Don't worry. We thoroughly clean and cook the deer that we catch. If you aren't comfortable eating that we do also have cow, pig, and chicken if you like. We prefer growing or raising our own food rather than buying it from a store. We don't really trust stores, especially commercial ones since they mostly are run by vampires." Grimsley explains once again.

"So many things going on here. So many of these things are normal for them but so strange for me," I thought. "How could I adjust to a life like this quickly enough?"

I and Grimsley came to a stop in front of two large oak doors that look like the doors you see at a old castle in Europe. They creak from age as Grimsley pushes them open with ease and inside I see it almost looks like a warehouse in a way. There are high ceilings with fans vrooming and high windows that streaks of sunlight are sneaking through, adding to the warehouse look. Pendent lights hung in equal parts which provided more light that reflects on the black wooden floors that were covered with blue mats that you see in a gym. In the center of the big room was a pole and behind it a few others along with a wall of mirrors where I saw a latina woman standing with a exercise bra and tights.

She had thick, jet black hair with streaks of vibrant red up in a high ponytail. She had a even tan and toned body. She was about my height and when we got closer I saw she has bright brown eyes which at first looked angrily at Grimsley but then soften when she switched her eyes over to at me.

"This is Ember," Grimsley said while motioning over to her.

"I think she knows who I am Grimsley." said Ember in a thick accent, she growled out Grimsley's name; clearly she wasn't fond of him. She looks over at me and gives me a soft smile. "I heard you want to learn self-defense. Will I'm your woman to learn it."

"I'll let you two train. I need to talk to alpha about the recent rogue issues." Grimsley nods to Ember who just gives him a stone cold look and turns to me. "I'll be back in a bit." He looked as if he wanted to say or do something else but wasn't sure what it was for a bit before giving me a small smile and leaving, closing the door behind him.

"We'll be starting off with something that many wouldn't dream of doing for agility. Pole dancing." Ember leads me over to the poles that were in the center of the room.

~

"Well, I found out which pack Cello is from. He's from the Stone pack. Makes sense, they never liked Cello being talked about," said Marshall.

I, Grant, Marshall, and Valentine had decided to do some of our own research into the rogues to see if we could figure out why they planned this attack on Accalia. I was sitting at Alpha's desk, flipping through paperwork and reports while Valentine and Grant were sitting on the floor, going through a chest of old, yellowing papers; Marshall was sitting in a corner of the room, doing research in the online archives.

"Isn't the Stone pack the pack that had that crazy cult crisis?" Asked Valentine, not looking up from the paper he was looking at.

"Ya. All but one member had committed suicide, a 5 year old girl who was locked in her bedroom. I guess they wanted her alive to continue the cult's legacy," said Grant. I felt a wave of guilt hit me at the mention of suicide; thinking about how I had made Accalia attempt suicide and then instead of chasing after her like Zarik wanted me to I chose to block him out and continue flirting with her sister. Hoping I could forget the sight of a beautiful white wolf running past me. Whenever I kissed her all I could think about was the broken look in Accalia's eyes and how mystical she looked in her wolf form.

"I remember hearing how her parents were actually human but had joined the cult in hope of becoming werewolves themselves. They offered their daughter as a sacrifice to the leader who turned the daughter down but since he didn't have a daughter of his own, decided to make her his daughter," said Valentine, breaking me out of my thoughts. I and Grant acknowledge looks before I look at Valentine.

"How did you hear about that? No one knew that information but the Stone pack and Alpha." I look up from the paper I was looking at to look directly at Valentine. This happened about 20 years ago, Valentine wouldn't have even been born yet and by the time he was born, the cult was no longer major news.

"Kids at school. Anyways, when can we done? I promised Zach I play capture the flag with him later," said Valentine.

"Not until we find out who those other wolves are." said Marshall, clicking away at a laptop. Valentine just pouted but started flipping through papers again, this time purposely throwing them at Marshall who was on the floor in a corner, some hitting him on the face.

"Hey Maddox just got back with me. He said he and Dante had gotten into a fight one night and Dante stormed off, he hasn't been seen since. It's only been a week and Dante hasn't shown up in the news yet so he just figured he was taking a while to cool off and didn't want to talk to anyone. It wouldn't be the first time Dante done this as he has a history of isolating himself." Said Grant while scrolling through his phone.

"What was the fight about?" Asked Marshall, putting the papers in a neat stack next to him just for Valentine to throw more at him.

"I guess Dante was promised the beta position but then their alpha changed her mind and decided to choose Maddox instead for unknown reasons," said Grant.

"There's rumors that Maddox had slept with her to gain that position. She is well known for messing around," said Valentine.

"Once again, why do you know this?" I asked.

"Rumors. Anyways, how is sleeping with someone going to help you gain a position? And how is she messing around? Is she playing with the little kids a lot?" Valentine went back to his naive state.

"It wouldn't be the first time there were rumors around her. Julia isn't exactly the most innocent alpha. Bleu doesn't like her because of how she acts and Vera is just judgemental of everyone." Said Marshall, having given up on trying to keep the papers in a neat stack and now is just throwing them into a pile.

"Hey guys, remember how Grayson and Devin were potentially framed?" I said.

"Ya. What about it?" Asked Grant.

"Will apparently this isn't the first time they were framed. When they left and were accepted into the Fabled pack, members from the Cave pack were committing crimes under their name. They would do crimes ranging from petty robbering to even murder of a human and a vampire. The wolf doing the murder claimed that the vampire was about to attack the woman was simply protecting but she ran away and fell down a hill, killing her." I read off of a report from the Cave pack. "The name of the wolf is Fletcher Burns."

"I remember that case. It was heavily divided as both the Cave and Fabled packs were claiming innocence and accusing the other. The Cave pack went as far as to say that the government was targeting them for banishing Grayson and Devin and favoriting the Fabled pack," said Grant.

"Will apparently he and Grayson are twins. That's why it was so speculated and Grayson was seen in the area earlier that day. The only way you could tell them apart was through their voices and Grayson has more scars on his body than Fletcher. The woman could not identify either's voices and it was dark so she couldn't see any scars. Eventually Fletcher confessed after being caught assaulting another vampire," I said.

"That would explain why he's using Grayson's name. But who could Devin be? Accalia said they appeared to be family members right?" Said Marshall.

"I can't find anything else about their family. Both parents passed a year ago and there doesn't appear to be any other living relatives," I said.

"Maybe Fletcher is also gay," said Grant.

"It could be possible I suppose. I'll get in contact with Grayson and see if he can tell me anything," I said.

"Hey remember how Jet Corvids was banished from his pack? Will apparently the man he killed was the brother of his mate, Amelia Harp. Amelia claimed her brother abused her and had a history of drug abuse and gambling. She had called him to tell him that their father died in a car accident and he needed to be there. Jet never been to a gambling den before so it's unusual for him to suddenly go to one. Some speculate that Amelia put him up to it. After he was banished, Amelia went with him," said Grant.

"But Amelia's human. She can't be a werewolf," said Valentine.

"No. But she could be the mastermind behind the ambush. She could be upset that Jet was banished so she came up with the plan to ambush Accalia to lure Grimsley," said Marshall.

"What do we know about her?" I asked.

"She was a high-ranking scientist in some sort of biology laboratory. They got shut down for illegal testing of animals and possibly humans as well. She claimed innocence and took a deal to avoid major jail time. After the trial she disappeared without a trace," said Grant.

"Why would she create this huge ambush though? And how would she have known about Accalia?" Said Grant.

"A lot of the other packs know about Accalia. Word spreads quickly," said Valentine.

"But how would she get Dante, Fletcher, Cello, and that other wolf to go along with her plan? Jet would of been easy and Cello already dislikes us so it wouldn't be hard to persuade him. But what about Dante and that unknown wolf?" I said.

"Maybe she promised Dante something? It could be possible they all have a grudge over a pack and agreed to help each other out in getting revenge," said Marshall.

"But why allow themselves to be captured by us? Why not resist or scream insults at us?" I said.

"I...I don't know. Maybe the unknown wolf will give us the answers we need," said Marshall.

"If we can find their identity. There has to be another relative of Grayson's and Fletcher's. That or Grayson knew something about Fletcher's mate," said Grant.

"What if they aren't relatives?" Said Valentine. We all look at him, encouraging him to continue. "Fletcher left his pack right? Will what if he was asked to leave? Grayson did talk about how their family is very strict and focused on their reputation, they completely cut him off as they saw him as an embarrassment. What if Fletcher's family did the same thing and eventually the pack? The reason we are no longer having reports on them could be because Fletcher and those 4 did something to them? Take down one pack by one."

"That would make sense. Attacking a vampire is already a huge embarrassment so having done it twice would easily lower anyone to omega level," said Marshall. "He's the only one in the pack who attacked vampries right?"

"According to the report, yes. There's been arguments between the pack and vampires, but none of them led to a fight as big as Fletcher's," I said.

"Guess it's settled then. We make a trip to visit the Cave pack and see what's going on there," said Marshall. I open my mouth to object but then decide against it. Marshall already made the decision.

Accalia

"Wow. You're pretty good at this, senorita. Where did you practice?" I and Ember were sitting on some wooden benches to relax after the training and pole dancing that she had me do.

"I had a lot of free time since I had no friends and my parents didn't watch me. I would often go climbing trees in the forest and sometimes if I wasn't paying attention a bear would track me down so I had to climb high and quick. I eventually learned how to bend my body so then I can fit in small crevices where they couldn't get me. I also learned how to be flexible when running through trees and having to avoid branches," I explained.

"You never actually did gymnastics or pole dancing?"

"Sometimes after school I would practice in the gym. The teacher didn't care as long as I didn't make a mess or brake anything. We have a gymnastics team so after practice the coach would let me practice as long as I put everything back and clean up."

"Wow. I wish I had as much free time as you did. If I'm not training these dummies then I'm spending my time practicing my own moves or teaching a class." Ember took another sip of her water.

"It's nice I guess. No one paid attention so I really just got to do whatever I wanted. At times I did wish I had someone to join me. It gets lonely when you're always by yourself," I said.

"I hear ya. I wish we would of met sooner. I feel like we got a lot in common," said Ember.

"Heh, ya. It would of been nice to have someone helping me climb a tree when I'm trying to avoid being mauled by a bear," I said.

"Will if it makes you feel better, bears don't really trespass into the territory. They kinda avoid us and we respect them. Just don't get near a mother and her cubs. Grimsley was once dared to try and pet a cub by Grant and he nearly got mauled by her if it weren't for Luna stepping in and calming her down. Luna has a way to calming down anyone and anything. Even angry mother bears."

"Why would he agree to it?"

"Because he was stupid? He isn't really his own person you know? He's kinda whatever people want him to be. His father wants him to be a ruthless and emotionless alpha so he plays that role. Luna wants him to express his interests and pursue them so he starts painting and drawing like crazy. At your school they want him to be the stereotypical jock so he does every sport imaginable. Teachers want him to be a model student so he aces every class and takes every honors or AP class there is. He's never truly doing something that HE wants you know?"

I think about all the times I've had a class with him. I would see him sleeping in the middle of class or not paying attention at all but when a teacher holds him back after class he's suddenly alert and answering every question that is being asked. When I've hung out at the bleachers I would see him at football practice and then later that same day he was running around the track until dusk.

"I guess you're right," I mutter to myself.

"Rethinking your decision of accepting his rejection?" chimes in Orchid.

"No. I'm just thinking about how stressful that would be. Constantly changing yourself to meet someone else's ideal idea of you. Never being able to do what you truly want or allow yourself a moment to relax, constantly on edge for being that ideal person."

"Ember did mention his mother encouraged him to pursue his interests which it sounds like art was his interest," said Orchid.

"Ya but I never saw him step foot in the art room. The only time I saw him there was to ask the teacher something and then leave immediately after."

"You spent a lot of time on school grounds even after school right? Maybe he was doing that as well."

"Maybe..." The doors opening brought my attention to Grimsley who has a grim look on his face. He looked stressed and tired but at the sight of I and Ember he quickly covered it up with a look of alertness and straightened his posture.

"I'm assuming training went fine," said Grimsley.

"Si. You got one flexible amor here. I and Accalia are going to have to meet up again sometime and really get to know each other. Si, senorita?" said Ember turning to face me with a warm smile on her face.

"Si," I said.

"I'll take you to meet Avery. He'll be helping you lift weights," said Grimsley.

"Don't be afraid of big old bad Avery. He's a softie with a booming voice. Could easily crash your skull if he so chose," said Ember, glaring over at Grimsley after she said that.

"Thanks..." I said before following Grimsley out of the room.

"Accalia, I'm going to have to go for a bit. The Cave pack seemed to have mysteriously vanished and we think they may have the unknown rogue that Fletcher was seen with. Fletcher was Grayson's twin brother," said Grimsley. "I'll make sure you have your own room and accommodations. I'll let the servants along with the members know that you have full range of the packhouse. While I can't make Ember stay her sister, Magnolia will be and Magnolia already agreed to helping you with anything you need."

"You mean Magnolia Lopez? The most popular girl at the school?" I said, shocked.

"Yes. Ember isn't exactly the only wolf here who hates me. Magnolia immediately told me no when I asked her for a favor but when I explained it to her she was more than happy to help," said Grimsley.

"What if I want to go with you?" I stop walking and Grimsley turns around to look at me, giving me a shocked expression.

"It's too dangerous. We don't know what we're walking into nor who is there. There's a possibility that vampires have taken over and are planning a ambush. That area is crawling with vampires who wouldn't hesitate to attack a wolf, especially a wolf from the royal pack," said Grimsley.

"I'm already good at agility, Ember said so herself and Avery can help me gain more muscle and I can learn how to fight," I argue back.

"I'm not allowing it. It's too dangerous. I know I fucked up once but I'm not fucking up again. Please Accalia, let me keep you safe. I've endangered your life one too many times now," Grimsley began to sound desperate, begging even.

"I can do it Grimsley. I'm not some helpless teenage girl like you think I am, I am a inferno and nothing can put us out," I and Orchid said together. Grimsley flinched at both of us talking and he looked to be debating about what to say next.

"Let me think about it. I have to check with alpha about the circumstances." With that, Grimsley turned around and continued walking. "I'll take you to Avery for right now."

We were walking down long hallways once again but now these were filled with portraits or either wolves or people, some painted while others photographed. They each had a year above them along with names in cursive writing on a golden plaque and a golden frame.

"These are the ancestors of my family. The wolves are the alphas and lunas and the people are aunts, uncles, cousins, etc." explained Grimsley, not bothering to turn around and look at me. I can tell from his body language and tone of voice that he isn't happy with me.

"Grimsley. I can take care of myself. I'll be surrounded by trained wolves anyways," I said, hoping he would agree to letting me go.

Grimsley suddenly turns around sharpy and I almost run into him; he doesn't flinch nor does he do anything to stop me, he just simply stands there and stares at me with a emotionless expression. "I said let me think about it. Just because you'll be surrounded by others doesn't mean they won't pick us off easily or find ways to capture you without alerting us."

"What if I stick by your side then? You saw me fighting those rogues, I can fight some vampires. They're just fast and strong right?"

"Don't underestimate a vampire. A vampire can easily kill a unprepared wolf, a group of them can take down a alpha as well if there's enough of them against one. Just because there's going to be a group of us doesn't mean we can easily overpower them. We don't know how old they are or how many there are of them. We're going into vampire territory where there are multiple clovens of them residing. This isn't some small sidequest, this is a major expedition."

"Please Grimsley. If you want to make up to me for what you did, then let me come with you. I'm no use if I just sit here and do nothing but train and whatever. I can easily do that anyday. I want to prove myself to the pack." I argued back, keeping my tone neutral to avoid sounding desperate.

"I'll let you know my decision by nighttime. Avery is waiting." Grimsley didn't bother to wait for a response from me and continued walking, leaving me standing there.

~

"This is Avery. He'll be training with you as well." Avery easily towered over Grimsley with being at least 6 feet tall and heavy built. He has rich ebony skin and a military hair style along with scars all around his face, one long scar that hit the corner of his left eye and went all the way down his face caught my eye. His eyes held a soft warmth to them and his hands could easily cover half a basketball in each hand. Ember saying he is huge was an understatement, he was the definition of a body builder.

"So this is the famous Accalia. Nice to meet you, madam." Avery's voice was loud and booming, hard not to miss and not listen to. His hands were covered in scars as well and felt rough when I shook them, his hand completely encompassing mine.

"Hi...sir," I said nervously.

"Heh. Don't be afraid. Many look at me and immediately think I'm a hitman or gang member. Truth is, I was in the military, did all branches but airforce. I couldn't fit in the airplanes." Avery let out a good chest filled laugh at that and it felt as if the entire room was shaking from the rumbling of his laughter.

"I once again won't be able to stick around. I'll come by to grab you and show you the food court." Grimsley left without saying another word.

"Something happen between you two? Grimsley doesn't exactly seem thrilled to be having your presence once again," said Avery.

"No...just a small disagreement between us is all," I said, not wanting to get into the details.

"Not my place to poke around, I'm just here to train you. So let's start," said Avery.